From Dance Class to Dream Date

"Daphne said I should come over someday, and she'd teach me how to play tennis. Do you think I should go?"

"Of course you should, stupid!" I was tired of hearing about Daphne, and my irritation was beginning to show. "Look, she was practically asking you to make a date with her."

Stanley looked glum. "Do you think it'll ruin my chances with her that I didn't?"

There was a clang from the triangle, signaling that it was time to dance. I felt bad that I'd put him down. "You shouldn't worry so much, Stanley. I keep telling you, you have everything. Good looks, intelligence, coordination, personality."

Stanley reacted to my compliments with grateful surprise. He seized me in the tango grip and I snuggled comfortably into his embrace. *Wait till Daphne gets the wonderful feeling of being held by him,* I thought. *She'll be his forever. And where will that leave me?*

Partners

Emily Hallin

AN ARCHWAY PAPERBACK
Published by POCKET BOOKS

New York   London   Toronto   Sydney   Tokyo

AN ARCHWAY PAPERBACK *Original*

An Archway Paperback published by
POCKET BOOKS, a division of Simon & Schuster Inc.
1230 Avenue of the Americas, New York, NY 10020

ISBN: 0-671-68359-4

First Archway Paperback printing September 1989

10 9 8 7 6 5 4 3 2 1

AN ARCHWAY PAPERBACK and colophon
are registered trademarks of Simon & Schuster Inc.

Printed in the U.S.A.

IL 6+

Partners

AT FIRST I couldn't believe I was seeing Stanley Stoneman. He was pacing the hall outside the multipurpose room. He would approach the door, turn back, and then pace again, as if making up his mind whether or not to go in. He must have decided against it, for he began to retreat, an expression of desperation on his face.

But I was blocking his getaway. When he saw me, his desperation turned to panic. He reversed course and plunged right through the doors of the multipurpose room. The scene amazed me, not only because I had frightened Stanley away but also because of who he was. Practically the last person I would have expected to see at the town recreation program's ballroom-dancing class.

I'd had second thoughts about entering the room myself, but now curiosity to follow up on Stanley sent me speeding through those swinging doors.

There couldn't be anyone else like Stanley. "Stone Face," the kids at school called him. He was a senior, a year ahead of me, pretty much a loner, and considered to be a super snob. "He thinks he's too good to be seen with us," one of my friends had said one day when we passed his rigid figure walking alone in a hallway at school.

"Wouldn't you, if you were in his shoes?" Lee Ann Adams, my best friend, asked. "His father was in *Wealth* magazine as one of the twenty-five richest people in California."

My friends and I had never even seen the Stonemans' house. It had so much land around it that practically a whole forest of trees and bushes hid it from view.

No wonder I was shocked to see such an elite person bumbling around at the Community Center.

The Community Center was an abandoned grade school. Some schools in our town had been closed because there weren't so many children now. So, what was once Hillview Elementary School was now the Community Center. The multipurpose room had doubled as an auditorium and cafeteria. I had gone to Hillview, and the multipurpose room held a lot of memories for me. I could still smell the bologna and peanut-butter sandwiches, oranges, and little waxed cartons of chocolate milk, and recall the feathery feel of biting into a Twinkie. I had been in a play there once, and I remembered being scared before my cue to come onstage.

But the people who filled the multipurpose room that September night bore no resemblance to the kids from my grade school days. There was a couple as old as my grandparents. The man was reed-thin, with eyebrows that jutted out at right angles, as if they were trying to escape being part of their meek and docile owner. His companion—his wife, I guessed—made three of him: a stout, heavy-legged, rosy-cheeked woman with an unvarying smile that seemed to be glued on.

A younger couple, probably in their twenties, looked enough alike to be brother and sister, but obviously weren't because of the way they were flirting and giggling. They were tall enough to be teammates on a basketball team.

Everyone seemed to be in couples. I wondered if I should have come alone. The announcement of this class had said, "Couples recommended." Recommended and required were different, so I had assumed it was okay to come alone. Yet, of course, I couldn't do ballroom dancing without a partner. I began to feel embarrassed about being alone. Stanley Stoneman seemed to be the only other single person. That was even more humiliating.

Other couples arrived. Most of them looked married and much older. Stanley, still appearing desperate and apprehensive, had his eyes fixed on the door. Maybe he was expecting a partner. A thirtyish lady in a tent dress and huaraches came through the door. She couldn't possibly be Stanley's partner, but I looked at him for a reaction. What I saw on his face was a kind of terror. Then he made a quick move toward me, almost hiding behind me.

A gulp emerged from his throat first, followed by a

question, forced out with considerable effort. "Did you come with anybody?"

"No."

"Most of the people here seem to have partners. Maybe you and I ought to team up, being the only ones our age."

"Why not?" I shrugged. Obviously he only chose me as the lesser of two evils. "If we don't have partners, the teachers will have to dance with us," I added.

The teachers had arrived and they were bustling around in a corner of the room, setting up a tape deck and sorting through their tapes. The woman teacher had jet-black hair that had been shaped into a stiff helmet. She wore a name tag that said "Mrs. Kriek."

"I wouldn't want to dance with the dragon lady," Stanley said.

The man teacher wore preppy clothes, and his blond curly hair could have been permed. "Mr. Fancher," his name tag read.

A beanpole of a fortyish man with a kind of small head entered the room just then and we watched him in silence.

"Yes, let's definitely team up," I finally said. "No other kids our age are coming."

Stanley glanced around at the people in the hall. "Looks that way," he said. "It makes me feel out of place. Though I should have known. The flier said this was an adult class."

Neither of us spoke for a few minutes. Then, curious as to why Stanley was there, I led off by saying, "Maybe you wonder why I signed up."

Stanley gave me a look that said he didn't really care. I went ahead and told him anyway.

"I wouldn't have wanted to learn this kind of dancing, but my grandma and grandpa are going to have their golden-wedding-anniversary party at the Elks Club in November, the Sunday night after this class ends. And I thought it'd be neat if I could dance with my grandpa. Nobody knows I'm in this class, not even my mom or dad. They think I'm in Japanese brush painting. Grandpa will be so surprised that I can do something like the waltz."

Stanley cast a pained grimace my way. "Yeah, I'll bet."

Mrs. Kriek emerged from the corner of the room and struck a metal triangle with a bar, and we all focused on her.

"I believe we're all here," she said. "But just to be sure, I'll call out your names."

She went through the list in alphabetical order, and I was surprised to hear Stanley Stoneman answer to the name of Richard Linton. He gave me a sideways glance after he replied. He must have seen my astonishment because he colored, looked away, and became rigid and unresponsive. He didn't even react when my name, Megan Royce, was called. He wasn't interested in my name or anything else about me.

"Before we begin to dance," Mrs. Kriek announced, "we'll go through a few fundamentals. The most basic aspect of ballroom dancing is posture. Everybody! Heads up! Stand as tall as you can. Pull in that stomach. Relax your shoulders. Now, face your partner. Move in till you're six inches apart. Good!"

Mr. Fancher faced Mrs. Kriek and now he took over the instructions. "Gentlemen." His voice rang through the room. "Place your hand on the lady's back." He illustrated, grabbing Mrs. Kriek below the shoulder blade. "Keep your fingers and thumb together."

"Ladies, rest your arm on your partner's, with your fingers on his shoulder." Mrs. Kriek demonstrated the move.

Stanley reluctantly plastered a limp hand on my back. I draped my arm over his, feeling I was intruding.

"Now, gentlemen, take the lady's right hand in your left, holding it between your thumb and index finger."

Mr. Fancher and Mrs. Kriek, after demonstrating the handhold, separated and made the rounds of the room, correcting us.

"Firmly. Hold her firmly," Mr. Fancher instructed Stanley, moving his hand up against my back and pushing up his drooping elbow so that I could rest my arm on his.

"Now." He adjusted our hands. "Your palms should face forward, your thumbs crossed. It's important to establish the correct handhold in the beginning to keep you on track in some of the intricate maneuvers we'll do later.

"Here, get that elbow back. When you shove it forward like that, look what happens to your girlfriend. Her elbow gets pushed way back. Hold your hand up here, just even with her cheek, and relax." Mr. Fancher moved on to readjust another couple.

Stanley looked petrified. My fingers felt frozen to his shoulder. I got the message that ballroom dancing was going to be an ordeal rather than the fun I had expected. Stanley was in agony with his arm around me and holding my hand. It was humiliating for us both, but we had to stand in that embarrassing position while our teachers made the rounds of the other students.

"This is known as the closed position," Mr. Fancher announced when everyone was arranged to his satisfaction. Stanley remained rigid, looking over my head. I couldn't see over his shoulder, so I concentrated on keeping my hands in position.

"Now, let's do what we all came here for. Let's dance," Mrs. Kriek said. "We'll start with a waltz. The important thing is to listen and time your steps to the music."

Mr. Fancher made a final inspection of our feet, instructing the women to keep theirs a little to the right of the men's.

"We've heard those jokes about the clumsy man trampling all over his partner's feet," Mr. Fancher continued. I felt a slight tremor pass through Stanley and transmit itself out through our tensely clasped hands.

"You'd better not do that to me," I said, trying to lighten things up.

Stanley only gave me a nervous glance. Mrs. Kriek sounded the metal triangle once again, and Mr. Fancher pulled out a portable blackboard and revealed a design of red and white footprints, the red representing the left foot and the white the right foot.

"This is the basic waltz block, arranged in a square," he said. "We'll go through this a few times, and then we'll be ready to waltz."

"This is the dance I probably need to know most," Stanley muttered, more to himself than to me.

"Gentlemen!" Mr. Fancher ordered. "Step forward on the left foot, then step forward on your right foot. Bring your left foot up to your right foot. . . ." He went on describing the complicated waltz box.

There was laughter and groaning as we all attempted the figures.

"Step and step, three, four, five, six," Mrs. Kriek's voice instructed us.

"Ready for the music?" Mr. Fancher punched the tape-deck button and the strains of a waltz surrounded us.

"Step, sway, one, two, feet together." Mrs. Kriek kept time to the music.

Stanley was all nerves. I watched as little beads of sweat formed along his hairline. He clomped his way through the basic block, pushing and dragging me along in reverse, his feet grazing and colliding with mine from time to time. The tall couple bopped us from the side and laughed.

"Sorry," the tall man said, grinning.

I wished Stanley could be as casual about it.

Mr. Fancher was speaking again. "If we all progress counterclockwise around the room, we won't have any clashes," he said. "Now, Mrs. Kriek and I will lead the way, and you just enjoy yourselves."

"Yeah, I can imagine." Stanley gave a bitter groan. We followed directly behind the instructors, with the elderly couple behind us.

"Remember to listen to the music," Mrs. Kriek reminded us as she and Mr. Fancher swirled away. Stanley and I stumbled behind.

"We're getting it," I said in my brightest voice when we had performed three perfect waltz blocks and were staying ahead of the couple behind us.

"Maybe," Stanley conceded.

Viewing the class from around Stanley's arm, I informed him, "There are a lot worse dancers than we are."

Stanley's rhythm improved with that assurance, and when the number ended, Mrs. Kriek announced that we could take a breather.

"Mix and get acquainted with one another," Mr. Fancher suggested.

The elderly couple behind us advanced toward us eagerly. "I'm surprised to see such young people at this class," the lady said. "Teenagers today don't seem to dance together. I thought they just did those wild rock dances by themselves."

"I'm learning ballroom because I'm going to my grandparents' golden-wedding-anniversary party," I said.

"I bet you're wondering why we old duffers are taking lessons at our age," the man said.

"We're going on a Caribbean cruise," his wife burst out. "There'll be a live band playing songs from the forties."

9

"It's our first cruise," the man said. "A whole week. We'll be dancing every night."

"Of course, we used to dance when we were young," the woman said. "But we haven't danced in twenty-five or thirty years."

The man laughed loudly. "You might say we're rusty, ready for a refresher course."

"At least you've done it before. We're rank beginners," I said. I wanted to kick Stanley—he hadn't said a word.

"I'm sitting down," he said to me in a low voice that definitely excluded the older couple. He made for a row of chairs against the wall.

I was absolutely fuming inside at Stanley's rudeness, and I wanted to let him know about it. "See you," I said to the couple, who had started a conversation with someone else. The kids at school were right—Stanley was impossible. I followed him, becoming more and more resentful of his attitude.

Stanley stood beside one of the chairs until I sat down, and then he plopped down beside me with a pained expression.

"It's not that bad!" I whispered angrily. "Loosen up and quit making this such a chore. You might accidentally find yourself enjoying it."

Stanley permitted his carefully controlled face to express amazement at my scolding.

"There's something I'd like to know," I asked, continuing to bug him. "What's the big idea of calling yourself Richard Linton?"

Stanley became pale, obviously stricken. "You know who I am."

10

"Of course I do. Doesn't everyone at Hillview High?"

"Am I that conspicuous?"

"I don't know about you, but your father is pretty famous. Anyway, that shouldn't give you an excuse to use an alias."

"I did it because people always connect me with him. I thought that here nobody would know me, but it turns out that you knew he was my father all along."

"Well, it doesn't matter to me who your father is. You can be as anonymous as you want."

"That's something, anyway." He retreated into his misery, resting his elbows on his knees, his face on his upturned hands, staring at the floor.

I caught a scent of musky perfume from a petite, thirtyish woman who strolled in front of us, talking about business with her partner. I guessed they worked in the same office. I heard raucous laughter from the tall, gangly couple. The rest of the class mingled and socialized while Stanley and I languished in silence. I tried to draw him out. I'm known as a nonstop gabber.

"I was wondering why you happened to come to this class," I began, drawing only a stare from Stanley.

"Those older people are going on a cruise, and I'm going to my grandma and grandpa's golden anniversary. I thought you might have some reason, too."

Stanley took a while to answer, letting me know with his silence that it was none of my business. All the time his eyes were darting around the room searching for an escape route. Then with a shrug of resignation he finally said, "I have to be an escort at the debutante cotillion." He looked down at the ground, and then he shot a reproachful glance at me. "Do you know what that is?" he asked, challenging me.

"Yes, I know what it is," I answered sarcastically. "Cotillion is just a fancy name for a big dance, and a debutante is a girl who's entering society."

He obviously didn't notice how sarcastic I sounded, because he continued, "It's ten weeks from last Saturday. They do a lot of this kind of dancing at the cotillion."

I continued my ruthless quiz. "But why this class? Don't they have private classes—for people going to cotillions?"

"Sandra Elliot's School!" Stanley sounded scornful. "I'm not going there. All the others go there, probably even Daphne Wainwright, whom I have to escort. I can't let her see what a klutz I am before the cotillion. This way, maybe I can get good enough—though I'm beginning to doubt it—that she'll never have to know. Even if Daphne isn't at Elliot's, other kids would be there and they'd tell her about her geek escort."

"Daphne Wainwright must be pretty special."

"You can say that again!" Stanley's reserve broke a little and his eyes seemed to come alive.

I noticed that when Stanley permitted his emotions to show, he was really good-looking. If the kids at school could see his reaction to Daphne Wainwright, who apparently went to some private girls' academy, they'd never call him Stone Face again.

Once started Stanley kept talking. "Not that I know

12

her that well. I've seen her recently, but that's about all since we were kids. In fact, she's so popular that I can't figure out why I was chosen as her escort." The spark disappeared from his eyes and they turned dull brown again. "Well, actually, I can figure it out. It's because of my dad—and his position."

With that, Stanley glared at me, outraged that I had dragged these confidences from him.

Mrs. Kriek sounded the triangle.

"I guess we might as well keep plugging away," Stanley said dismally.

Plugging was right. The waltz had a few variations that we learned after the intermission. For instance, the hesitation. Stanley kept losing his balance and I kept getting my left foot confused with my right. Then there was the twinkle, where our feet had to be crossed in front and in back of each other. We got so tangled up that Mr. Fancher had to come and unwind us.

Stanley and I ended up back to back instead of facing each other in the arch turn, and I got hysterical. Even Stanley indulged in a little snicker.

"We'll go over that again next session," Mrs. Kriek said with an acid glance in our direction.

2

AFTER HEARING ABOUT Stanley's escorting Daphne to the cotillion, I decided I should have an escort to the Elks Club for the anniversary party. I couldn't just dance with my grandpa or dad or little brother, Kevin, all evening. An escort would make the night special for me. I asked my mom if I would be expected to pass appetizers and carry dirty glasses to the kitchen.

'Of course you won't, Megan," Mom said. "The waiters will take care of that. You're just expected to have a good time and socialize with the guests."

I thought that over. Realizing that the guests were going to be mostly my grandma and grandpa's age, I knew I'd need an escort my age. I just wished there was someone to appoint an escort for me, as someone had assigned Stanley to Daphne Wainwright. But I didn't see that happening in my future, so I'd just have to ask my own date, maybe one of the guys I kidded around with in school. Just about anybody ought to be glad to go to a party where there were going to be miniature pizzas and quiches and tiny puffs filled with crab and chicken salad, pigs in blankets, and a yummy salsa dip, to say nothing of the special "wedding" cake that had been ordered.

The only problem was that I had never dated. Actually, I didn't have time for it. I was busy with all my other activities. I'm into sports—all sports. You name it, if there's an opening on a team, I'll join it. I jog and bike, and my girlfriends, Colleen Carter, Lee Ann Adams, and Thelma Arkadian, demand a lot of time, and besides, I love to talk, an activity that's best with girlfriends. Also, my grandpa and grandma are always after me to do some public service. "Every American citizen should perform some kind of help to others," they keep drilling into Kevin and me. Last year I was a Wildlife Rescue volunteer. I not only fed baby birds until they were ready to fly and took care of a wounded squirrel, but also helped keep records at the office. Grandma says that birds and squirrels deserve help as much as people.

This year I'll still work on that project, but not as much. Mrs. Gadsden, our home-ec teacher, has started a nursery for the babies of students who want to finish high school. She's offered extra credit to anyone in home ec who'll volunteer to help take care of the babies a couple of hours a week. Mine was the first hand up, and Grandpa was pleased about that.

"Those girls need all the help they can get," he said. "They've got to have a good education to raise those babies. They're hardly mature enough to be mothers."

So you see, I'm too busy to concentrate on boys. Still, I'm not shy around them, nor am I boy-crazy like some people I know. I am acquainted with quite a few guys in a casual way, though not well enough to invite them to an important social event.

I racked my brain for candidates. I thought that maybe Kent Whitehead might like to go. I'd known him since the year one. He used to be in my Sunday-school class and we went to the same church camp. At camp he took a lot of joking about his name, since he has coal-black hair.

Another possibility was Dennis Ridge. He does gardening for my grandparents, so actually he's more a friend of theirs than mine. I see him now and then when he's weeding their garden or mowing their lawn because my grandparents live next door to us. I'm not sure Dennis knows who I am. I've never spoken to him, but I guessed I could remedy that.

I was pretty sure that neither Kent nor Dennis knew how to do ballroom dancing, but if I asked one of them soon, maybe I'd be able to give him some quick instructions. I decided to practice on Kevin.

"Kevin, you ought to dance with Grandma at the anniversary party," I warned him.

"Phooey," he replied, just what you'd expect from an eleven-year-old.

"I'm serious. This party is a big deal for our family. It only happens once every fifty years. You have to keep this a secret, but I'm going to dance class so I can surprise Grandpa by knowing how to waltz. I'll teach you what I learn every week, so that way you can dance with Grandma. Even Mom and Dad will be surprised. Maybe you might even want to ask a date— how about Kathy Hamilton?"

Kevin's reaction to my suggestion was to turn brick red, matching his hair, and to make a raspberry sound with his tongue.

"You have to grow up sometime," I said. "Before long you'll be in high school. Besides, nobody has as neat a pair of grandparents as we have. Remember when Grandma and Grandpa took us on that trip to Colorado?"

Kevin's face lit up with the memory. "I remember that little train. I thought we'd crash into that canyon for sure."

"And remember those weird Indian houses in the cliffs?" I thought of the birds that flew over the ancient Indian village, and how Grandma knew the names and habits of all of them.

Grandma is the one who got me into Wildlife Rescue. She's also a volunteer. Grandma and Grandpa, living so close, are almost more like parents to us than Mom and Dad. Mom is a nurse and works a lot of weird hours. Dad has to work overtime a lot, but Grandma and Grandpa are always there. Kevin and I are lucky. We know a lot of kids who have only one parent, and we practically have four.

Grandpa isn't as interested in birds and animals as Grandma. You'd think people who had been married for fifty years would do everything together. But not Grandma and Grandpa. Grandpa, who was raised on a farm, is more interested in helping refugees from Southeast Asia than animals. He's teaching a group of these refugees how to farm U.S.-style. He took me out

17

to visit them once, and I was impressed how Grandpa and these people who didn't speak the same language could understand one another and could even laugh together.

Grandma and Grandpa don't even travel together all the time. Grandpa had been in the navy for a while and said he was traveled out. But Grandma would take off with some nature group for a South American jungle and then she'd come back home and make speeches all over town about saving the rain forest. Grandma and Grandpa usually go around in jeans and sweatshirts, and that was another reason their fiftieth wedding anniversary was going to be a gala occasion. Grandpa was going to rent a tuxedo.

I got off on a tangent about Grandma and Grandpa and their party when I was supposed to be telling about the ballroom-dancing class. Getting back to the subject, the next Tuesday night I wondered if Stanley Stoneman would show up for the second lesson. I was afraid he might have been discouraged by the waltz. But apparently his desire to impress Daphne Wainwright overcame everything, because he turned up. He looked surprised to see me, too. He ambled slowly to my side of the room.

"You braved it again," he said.

"I figured I needed a little more practice." I grinned at him.

He gave a little wince that could have been the start of a smile. "Yeah, a slight brushup is in order for me, too."

We just stood there, with silence mushrooming between us while I racked my brain for something interesting to say. Should we talk about Daphne Wainwright again? No, I preferred to bring up the subject of my escort.

"I have to get all the steps right tonight," I informed Stanley, "because whoever is going to escort me to my grandparents' party doesn't have a clue about ballroom dancing, and I'll have to teach him."

"That's not a great idea," Stanley said. "Number one: you haven't learned yourself. How can you teach someone else to dance? Number two: you're a girl, he's a guy. The steps are totally different. For instance, look at the diagram." From a folder Mrs. Kriek had handed to each of us he took out the diagram of footprints showing the arch turn. "Look how complicated it is for the man. The woman's part is simpler."

"I'll show him the man's diagram."

Stanley shook his head vigorously. "It'll never work. Why don't you just have him come to class with you?" Suddenly he looked distant, and his shoulders hunched up in a kind of shrug. He looked around the room with a pained expression, as if he wished he were alone.

I answered his question with disdain to match his. "How could I bring someone I haven't decided on yet? It's between two people. I can't decide which one should be my escort. Kent? I know him better. Or Dennis? He knows my grandparents better."

"Probably you ought to go with the one you like best."

"I can't say that I like one better than the other. They're totally different."

19

"Is one likely to be a better dancer than the other?"

"How should I know until I see them dancing?"

"Some dilemma." Stanley resumed his indifferent, bored expression, and I couldn't tell if he was sincere or not.

Mrs. Kriek jangled her triangle, and the class, which had now assembled, turned toward her.

"We all need more practice on the waltz, so we'll polish that up during the first half-hour," she said. "Then, in the last hour and a half you'll be introduced to the fox-trot."

We started out with the basic waltz block again, and to our surprise, we went through a dozen of those figures without mishap.

"Hey, we did it!" I exclaimed.

"Don't brag until we've mastered that arch."

"Right," I agreed. "Or those confusing twinkles."

But by some miracle and a lot of readjustment of our hands, ankles, knees, and elbows by Mrs. Kriek and Mr. Fancher, we even got those details ironed out.

"Don't grip her fingers so tightly," Mr. Fancher scolded Stanley when he was about to twist my hand off my arm. "Hold her fingers loosely so she has freedom to pivot."

Once Stanley's tense, damp hands relaxed, I could pirouette gracefully under the arch of our arms.

"You probably wish you were doing this with Dennis, or whoever," Stanley said.

"Too bad I'm not Daphne," I retorted.

Stanley frowned. "One reason it's important for me to master the maneuvers quickly is that I don't have as much time as I first thought. It turns out that although the cotillion is still weeks away, there are other events that I have to attend as Daphne's escort. For instance, a week from Saturday one of the debs' families is giving a tea dance.''

"A week from Saturday! That only gives you one more lesson! Well, if we get the waltz down perfectly, you could claim to be a waltz freak and sit out all other dances."

"Maybe I'll get a handle on the fox-trot, too." Stanley was a little short of breath now because we were going at a good clip around the line of dance.

When the music stopped, I gave Stanley a wide grin. "Do you realize that we danced a whole number without bumping into anybody? And we could talk while we were doing it."

"That's true." Stanley's face brightened.

"Daphne will really be impressed. You have natural coordination. You don't have to worry about that tea dance."

"Maybe not." Stanley smiled, looking out across the dance floor we had just circled.

"One thing I was wondering about," I said in the brief intermission during which Mr. Fancher got out the fox-trot tapes. "Since you belong to a crowd that has debuts and cotillions, why don't you go to a private school?"

"Good question." Stanley's face wore a triumphant smile. "Exactly the one my parents asked. 'Why would you want to go to Hillview High when we can send you to Broxton Academy?' The simple answer is that Broxton doesn't have a metal shop, but Hillview has an excellent one. It took a while to wear my parents down. They're both strong-minded. But I have both their genes combined, and when something is important to me, I can be more stubborn than the two of them together." A proud gleam animated Stanley's eyes, and he drew his shoulders up in a style that Mrs. Kriek approved of as perfect for executing the fox-trot, whose music was beginning to emerge.

Before Mrs. Kriek could put us back to work, I wedged in another question. "Why is the metal shop so important?"

"*Indispensable* is a better word. I'm an inventor. I'm interested in combinations of metal alloy, stress, and endurance of metal. In the future there are going to be metals we never heard of, mined from the ocean floor, maybe transported from space, and I'll be ready to devise uses for them."

Stanley was all worked up, and when Mrs. Kriek banged the metal rod on the triangle, the very material he was so freaked-out about strangled his lecture.

Mr. Fancher, over the mellow tones of a song, announced that we were starting with a slow version of the fox-trot. He demonstrated the footwork, slow, slow, quick, quick. Then he seized Mrs. Kriek, turned up the music, and they demonstrated.

"Gentlemen, left foot forward on the downbeat. One, two. A long, slow step on the right, three, four. Step to the side, right foot over, six. Stand tall, knees relaxed, no movement above the hips. Everybody, into position with your partner. One, two."

Mrs. Kriek and Mr. Fancher circulated. "As you step to the side, brush your foot against your ankle." Mrs. Kriek showed us how, and Stanley and I muddled through the first figure of the fox-trot. When we had reasonably mastered that basic step, we learned the variations. One was called the conversation. We turned into promenade position, and Stanley decided that this was a good time to start a conversation.

"Dennis who?" he asked.

"What?" I replied, and then I realized. "Oh, you mean the one who might be my escort. Dennis Ridge. But that's confidential. Actually, I don't know him very well. He goes to Hillview with us and he does gardening for my grandparents. Mainly I've just seen him over there sometimes. I wouldn't want the word to get out that I was considering him until I've decided he's the one."

It was a mistake for us to think we could talk and dance at this stage of learning the fox-trot. Stanley couldn't figure out how to remove us from the promenade position and back into line with the others. Mr. Fancher appeared, scowling and telling us to listen to the instructions. After the promenade we had to do the arch turn again, and I twirled easily under our hands.

"Daphne is just about as tall as you, I think," Stanley remarked. "Maybe a tiny bit shorter. I want to be sure we can do this like pros. I wouldn't want to tangle her up."

We worked on that group of steps until my ankles ached. Then, happily, Mrs. Kriek declared an intermission. We slumped into the row of folding metal chairs arranged along the wall. Next to us, a thirtyish couple sat down. The woman turned a toothy smile toward us.

"That was a workout," she remarked. "I'm Betty Potts and this is Jim." She gestured to her husband, who wore glasses and had a receding hairline. He leaned over her to socialize with us.

"This is more fun, less monotonous than the waltz," Jim interjected.

"That last one was good exercise, too," Betty said. "And we could use it." She gave a shrill laugh.

Stanley looked over at them, then tuned out.

"Jim and I looked through the adult-ed catalog and this is what we came up with," Betty said.

Jim leaned farther over her. "We were getting in a rut staying home and watching TV every night, and Betty said, 'Why don't we go out and take a course?'"

"Jim was in favor of ceramics."

"We would have had something to show for it, some vases or jars to put around the house," Jim said.

Stanley got up and wandered over to the water cooler. I was miffed that he hadn't asked me if I wanted to go with him and had just let me sit there by myself, being bored by Jim and Betty Potts.

Then it dawned on me that Stanley didn't have any obligation toward me. We weren't a couple, like Betty and Jim, but just two people who were thrown together because neither of us could dance alone.

"There was a time I favored the Chinese-restaurant tour," Betty said. "The chefs come out and tell you the history and ingredients of the different dishes at a new restaurant every week—but we have to watch the calories, and it was more expensive than this course. We have to get a baby-sitter, and that mounts up."

"But it's good for Betty to get away from Kenny and Jinny for a change."

"Real live wires." Betty took out her wallet and showed their pictures to me. "Jinny is just crawling, and Kenny is into everything. You can't leave a thing out that doesn't get broken. I'm one of those rare mothers who doesn't work."

"No need for her to. I make good money."

"He's the mechanic at Import Car Repair," Betty said, satisfied.

I looked at Stanley, who was strolling around the room. It wouldn't hurt him to be nice to somebody, but I had to admit I wasn't really fond of Betty and Jim's company either.

"This course is okay," Jim was rambling on, "but what'll we do with it after? Where will we dance?"

"We can roll up the rug and dance at home, honey," Betty said.

I could see Stanley pacing restlessly across the room. Mrs. Kriek's triangle sounded, and Stanley returned to me with a resigned sigh.

While Mr. Fancher was choosing the new tapes, Stanley turned to me with a halfway disinterested expression. "I've been thinking about this Dennis Ridge," he said. "It doesn't seem like a good idea to invite your grandparents' gardener to a social occasion in their honor."

3

I saw Daphne Wainwright's picture in the paper before the next class. Newspaper pictures are fuzzy, and it was difficult to tell exactly what she looked like. She was with thirty other debutantes lined up in three rows. There was also an article telling where they went to school, who they were, who their parents were, and who their escorts for the cotillion were.

It was right there in bold print in the paper: Daphne Wainwright, Crystal Creek School; parents, Mr. and Mrs. Lawrence Wainwright; escort, Stanley Stoneman. I wondered if Stanley was looking at the picture, too. I imagined his palms growing damp as he saw his fate in black and white; then he would assume a frown thinking of the responsibility of escorting Daphne Wainwright to the cotillion.

I wished I had a clearer view of Daphne, because I felt I had some responsibility in this matter, too. Stanley's skill as a dancing partner rested on my shoulders, or I guess I should say, my feet. Even in the blurred newspaper photo I could see that Daphne had a wide, self-confident smile with lots of even white teeth showing. She had lightish wavy hair that cascaded over one shoulder. She even had glamorous-looking high cheekbones. It was no wonder Stanley was so nervous about making a good impression on her.

How could he stand to drag me around the dance floor when he was destined for someone like Daphne? I never have time to fiddle with *my* hair. It's usually just tied back into an untidy ponytail with wisps straggling around the sides of my face, which happens to be moon-shaped and without a vestige of cheekbones. I've heard myself described as "wholesome."

It beats me why I cut out that picture and took it to school the next day. I guess it was because I was so involved in that debut myself, training one of the escorts to dance. I had that clipping in my purse when it was my turn to baby-sit in the school day-care center.

There were five babies in the small room next to the nurse's office that day. It used to be a supply room, and it was much too crowded for a nursery. There were four small cribs and a little play table with two children's chairs in bright red and yellow. A mobile with nursery-rhyme characters hung from the ceiling. My friend Thelma Arkadian was helping me tend the center for the hour.

Three of the cribs were full and one baby was in an Infanseat on the floor. The oldest baby, Gabriel, could pull himself up and hold on to the play table. Gabriel's

mother, Emerald Green, had just brought him in, and
he was fussing and whining and holding his arms out
to be picked up. I hoped he wouldn't wake the other
babies.

Emerald viewed Thelma and me with hostility. She
had a big chip on her shoulder and resented the people
who helped out in the day-care center.

"I'll hold him," I said. "I'll be on duty for the next
hour."

"Duty!" Emerald exclaimed with a sneer. "A lot
you know about duty. How would you like twenty-
four hours a day of it? You'd fold up quick as a flash.
Take him if you want. I'm about to be late."

She stalked out with a look that withered me. I don't
know why she was so belligerent and angry. She
always put me down, saying I only got involved in the
day-care center so I could get extra credit in home ec.
True, I did get extra credit, but I would have volun-
teered anyway.

Mrs. Gadsden told us volunteers how hard she had
to fight some of the school-board bigwigs and parents
who didn't think it was suitable for teenage mothers to
bring their babies to school. I agreed with Mrs. Gadsden that the mothers like Emerald Green needed to
finish high school so they could earn a living to raise
their babies. It was a cause I believed in, and besides,
I liked those babies. It always amazed me to see them
working at strengthening their bodies just so they
could turn over or lift their heads. That was as big an
accomplishment for those infants as it was for me to
learn to waltz.

Gabriel's accomplishments were especially spectacular. He was making sounds almost like words, and soon, I knew, he was going to say something.

"It's not fair for Emerald to insult us like that when we're helping," I said to Thelma, coming out of my daydream.

"Oh, well, we don't have to see her except for a few minutes. Besides, we get a lot out of taking care of these babies. My sister Rosemary said that when she took home ec they just had dolls that they'd bathe and change."

"You could never guess what it was like to take care of kids by practicing on dolls. These are wiggly, messy real people with wills of their own," I agreed.

"They're a lot of work," Thelma said, "but still I can hardly wait to have one of my own—after I get married, of course."

"Yeah, I feel sorry for these kids without any fathers."

"I'm not going to be much help today." Thelma hunkered down on the floor against the wall. "I have to study for a test next period."

"That's okay." I walked around, carrying Gabriel and his bottle until his eyelids started to droop. I put him in one of the cribs and he went to sleep.

The nursery became very quiet and I relaxed. It was Tuesday, the day of the dance class, and I scrabbled in my purse for the diagram of the footwork for the various fox-trot variations. The picture of the debutantes that I had cut out of the paper tumbled out with the diagram, and I took another look at Daphne Wainwright.

Poor Stanley. This would be his last lesson before

he had to face Daphne at a tea dance. Our lessons were far from complete. I'd do my best to make things smooth for him, to send him into society as polished as I could. One thing he had to learn was to make small talk with all kinds of people. I planned to scold him that night about his standoffish attitude.

Then I thought about teaching my prospective partner for the anniversary party to dance. Who would it be? Kent Whitehead might be a promising dancer. He was good at volleyball and at softball. He had long legs and was kind of skinny, about Stanley's height. There was only one thing about him that made me hesitate. He was hard to talk to. Dragging conversation out of Kent was frustrating and exasperating. I sat by him at dinner at camp sometimes and everything I started to say would be stymied by his self-conscious one-syllable replies. Then there would be silence while my brain got frazzled trying to think of something else to say. Maybe at the party there'd be so many people around, so much music and talk, that his silence wouldn't be so painful.

One of the babies stirred and cried out and I went to see what was the matter. It was tiny, only a few weeks old. Its hand fluttered up and it shifted a little and then lay still. I guessed it was having a dream. I wondered what such a young baby would dream about.

"Who was president when Florida became part of the United States?" Thelma surfaced from her books to ask.

"Polk," I said. "We had that last week."

The hour was over quickly, and I didn't make my escape before Emerald Green came back in to check on Gabriel. "Well, he's still alive after an hour with the extra-credit collectors." Emerald shot a look of pure hatred at Thelma and me.

Out in the hall Thelma said, "If it weren't for people like us, Emerald wouldn't be able to go to school at all."

"I guess she resents us because we can just walk out after an hour with Gabriel, while she's stuck with him for life. For about twenty years, anyway."

"And nobody to blame but herself," Thelma said in a snippy tone.

"Remember, Mrs. Gadsden said we weren't to be judgmental."

"She should tell that to Emerald."

Thelma and I parted and took off for our classes. Hurrying down the hall, I saw Dennis Ridge turning the corner at the end of the corridor. He wasn't as tall as Stanley; he was stocky and compact, making him look strong. I had seen him hauling huge bags of cuttings around my grandparents' yard. They swore he was very dependable, and he'd been doing their gardening since he was only fourteen.

"That boy has his head screwed on right," Grandpa had remarked once. "He's a good businessman, too. Used part of his earnings to buy himself a leaf blower to save time."

Dennis had a sincere, industrious look, and though I hadn't had a look at his eyes, I knew they must be blue, a good combination with sandy hair. Maybe I'd ask him. On his next gardening day, I planned to hang out at my grandparents' and find out if Dennis was easier to talk to than Kent. It was hard to imagine

31

Dennis dressed up and waltzing, but I only knew him as a worker. Grandma had warned me that you have to experience a person in some depth to know where he's coming from.

I expected Stanley to be tensed up that night at class. After all, in just four days he would confront Daphne Wainwright at a tea dance, and this was only our third lesson. Stanley was just as keyed-up as I'd expected. In fact, complications had arisen for him.

"I'm in big trouble," he announced to me as soon as I arrived.

But Mrs. Kriek sounded the triangle and I was kept in suspense about Stanley's problem for a while.

We reviewed the basic waltz, arch turn and all, and then we went through the "slow, slow, quick, quick" of the fox-trot. Stanley and I got mixed up again.

"My fault," I said. I didn't want him to lose confidence when his confrontation with Daphne was so near.

"I'm the one who stumbled," Stanley contradicted. His face looked grim. What was his problem? Had he had a run-in with Daphne?

Then we arrived at the variation of the fox-trot called the conversation, in which we were side by side, promenading. I hoped that Stanley would let me know his dilemma during that maneuver. Sure enough, he burst out with it.

"Our physics class is going on a field trip Saturday afternoon. It's positively vital to my future," he said, his voice choking with emotion.

"Saturday afternoon. Isn't that the same time as the tea dance?" I asked.

"Exactly!" He raised his hand to put me through an arch turn.

When I was facing him again, I had to shout over "Raindrops Keep Falling on my Head," "So you won't be able to go, will you?"

"To which?" he replied, grinding his foot down on my big toe, which protruded from open sandals.

"To the field trip," I said, masking my pain. "Aren't you already committed to the tea dance?"

"Yes, but that was before I knew what it would conflict with. Do you know where we're going on the field trip?"

"You never told me."

"To the Stars and Stripes Amusement Park."

"Attention. Couple four." Mr. Fancher looked in our direction. "It's fine to converse while you're dancing, but not to the extent that you miss the instructions, which you two seem to have done. Now, class, from the beginning, the Park Avenue, another variation of the fox-trot."

I wondered why the physics class would go to an amusement park until an intermission was called and we slid into a couple of folding chairs on the sidelines.

"Here's the idea." Stanley raked his hand eagerly through his dark hair and his eyes glinted. "We're going to ride the Tornado with some instruments to test the extragravitational force. And we have equations we have to solve, you know, with water bottles and weights—figuring out things like vertical acceleration. We'll work on the centripetal velocity on the

Tornado. And try to figure out why the designers made the Monster Loop the shape it is. You know a ride like the Monster Loop isn't perfectly round. If it were, the cars would slow down so much at the top that gravity could pull the riders out of their seats. Instead, they're made in a teardrop shape, in which the radius changes and controls the angular momentum of the cars.''

I couldn't understand any of what Stanley was telling me, but I did appreciate what changes all this scientific talk made in him. His cheeks glowed with some kind of new vitality. His hands described speedy circles and precipitous drops as he talked, making our animated fox-trot seem humdrum.

"Are you aware that the laws of physics may be totally overturned in the next decade?" His eyes bored into mine with an almost demonic intensity. "Scientists are beginning to challenge the Newtonian theory of gravity as a principal force in the universe. And all this is happening just as I'm coming onto the scene."

"Does this mean you're skipping the tea dance?"

"What else can I do? You see how important this field trip is. Mr. Grayson couldn't get the bus on a school day, so we have to go on Saturday."

"But isn't there supposed to be an equal number of guys and girls at the tea dance? Won't Daphne be all alone?"

Stanley looked miserable. "My mother will skin me alive. But Daphne won't be without a partner, because she's the star of that crowd. Anyway, I wasn't specifically supposed to be her partner at the tea dance. The only time I'm that is at the cotillion."

"I saw Daphne's picture in the paper," I said. "She's a knockout. You're lucky."

"I know. My mother is always harping about how I got the pick of the current crop of debutantes, and how I have to impress her. And here I'm going to miss out on the first party of the season."

"What if your mother makes you go to the dance?"

"I've got that all figured out. I'll tell her that if I don't go on the field trip I'll get so many points taken off my grade that it'll probably ruin my chances of getting into Stanford, where she wants me to go, although I'd prefer MIT."

"Well, then," I exclaimed just as we were summoned back to the dance floor by the sound of the triangle, "I guess you're not in such big trouble after all."

"It's still trouble," he assured me, "because my mother is going to be upset about it, and it might cause hard feelings with Barbara Gilliland, the hostess of the party, and with Daphne. I don't really know Daphne, and we should have gotten more or less acquainted at this tea dance."

We went into our routine, fox-trotting around the floor.

"We did okay on that. We're mastering all this footwork," Stanley said.

"I never knew the way you held your partner's hand was so important," I said. Our fingers had to be curled around each other's so Stanley could get the proper tension to swing me.

"That's true." Stanley began to glow again. "Maybe the laws of physics could be applied to the dance. For instance, how much torque do you have to apply to your partner's hand to get her to turn in the right direction? Do you think if I had an equation for that it would impress Daphne? I could bring an accelerometer and figure out how much centrifugal force she's taking when I twirl her."

I laughed. "I doubt it. She might be impressed with what a one-track nerd you are, and you'd turn her in the direction of some other guy. You want to make her think you're holding her hand in a certain way because you're entranced by the touch of her fingers. You have to be romantic instead of scientific. But you also have to get to the parties where she is. If you're not around, how can you impress her?"

"Don't worry. If I miss the tea dance, there'll be another party the next week. But anyway, it'll give me that much more time to perfect my technique."

"You're getting good," I said. "Really, you're so smooth, it's no effort at all to follow you. I know Daphne will think so."

"Have you decided which of those two guys you're going to ask to your grandparents' party?"

"No, I'm still deciding. This week I'm inclined toward Dennis Ridge, the gardener. My grandparents think he's great. I know it'd make them happy if he were at their party, and that's more important than who I want to go with. But I don't know him, and I thought I better get acquainted before I ask him. Just to make sure."

"It's the same way with Daphne and me. We don't really know each other that well. We've always gone to different schools, and I was with her only at the children's Christmas parties at the club. But we were so young then. Now that we're practically grown-up, it's a little bit overwhelming to suddenly be her escort at her debut.''

"I bet." I was memorizing the side of Stanley's face as I looked up at it—how his hair grew in a neat sideburn about halfway down the front of his ear. I pictured Daphne's feet where mine were. I imagined his hand on her back, propelling her into the arch turn we had mastered so well.

"YOU SHOULDN'T AVOID the other people in the class," I scolded Stanley when we stopped for the next intermission. "Whenever people approach us, you take off."

Stanley made a face.

"If you really want Daphne to think you're cool, you have to make other people think so, too," I continued. "Practice on these people so you'll be experienced at small talk. Then you can mingle at the cotillion. Even with Daphne's parents. Talk to some of the older people to practice."

Stanley gulped and looked terrified at the mention of Daphne's parents. "I'm not good at that kind of thing," he said.

"You weren't good at talking to me, either, when we started this class, but you were forced into it," I reminded him. "At the first session, you hardly said anything to me. I thought you were a real snob. Most kids at school still think so."

Stanley registered surprise, hurt, and anger. I had to reassure him quickly.

"Not that I think that now. I found out that you're an interesting and friendly guy. So would the kids at school, if you let them see what you're really like."

He sulked a little. I could have bitten my tongue for criticizing a person who needed to be built up.

"You're different," he said. "It's easy to talk to you. When I say something, you listen."

"So would the other people here. Or anybody at school. They'd soon forget who your father is."

Although Stanley produced a ghost of a smile, he stiffened a little at the mention of his father. I felt I had put my foot in my mouth again, so I took off for the ladies' room.

There I met the lady in the tent dress. She had on a personalized bracelet that said "Jerrolyn."

"You kids are really having a good time, aren't you? You're lucky to be learning with your boyfriend. Everybody here is a couple except me and my partner. People probably sympathize with him for having to drag such a lummox as me around. The only reason he came to this class is he just moved to California and thought he ought to get out and meet some people. And who did he have the bad luck to meet but me."

"Don't be so negative," I said. "Besides, Stanley—er, Richard—and I aren't a couple. We didn't even know each other until we came here." I told her why I had come.

"Well, I'm surprised!" she said. "You two are always deep in conversation, like old friends."

After the ill-advised lecture I had just given Stanley, that remark didn't seem appropriate.

"I joined the class as part of a self-improvement program," Jerrolyn confided. "I'm also on a diet. But I can't help feeling like an outsider in this class."

"Well, hey," I said, "why feel like an outsider? You paid your twenty-five dollars to learn to dance just like the rest of us. Maybe you haven't noticed, but nobody here is a candidate for Miss America or Mr. Universe. You're as good as anybody else, so why don't you quit hiding out in here and mingle? It's about time to start up again."

On my way out I wondered if there was something about me—maybe my trustworthy moon face—that made people spill their troubles to me and set me up to give advice. Maybe I'm fated to be a counselor or a psychiatrist or something.

I found Stanley talking to the fellow who was teamed up with Jerrolyn. I took a good look at him and decided he wasn't a prize package himself, and maybe he was lucky to have Jerrolyn. They made a pair like Jack Sprat and his wife. He was a beanpole with a smallish head with pale kinky hair and eyes that protruded a bit, as if there wasn't quite room enough for them inside his head.

"Congratulations," I said to Stanley when we got together for the next dance. "I saw you socializing with another class member."

"Glad you noticed," he said, gripping me in his

40

familiar manner, left foot forward, slow, slow, quick, quick.

Toward the end of the session, in which we had supposedly mastered the waltz and the fox-trot in all their variations, Mrs. Kriek asked all the men to form a circle facing in and the women facing out. Both circles were to move, and when the music stopped, you danced with whoever happened to be opposite you.

"When you go to a dance," she explained, "you'll probably change partners once in a while. You won't want to dance all evening with the same person."

"That doesn't apply to me," Stanley said, looking apprehensive as he linked hands with the other men. I wasn't too happy about the game, either. As the circle started to move, I surveyed the lineup and considered which of the men would be my partner. I hoped Stanley and I would just happen to be facing each other at the end.

As it turned out, I got the old gentleman who was going on the Caribbean cruise.

"Didn't you tell me you were learning so you could dance at your grandparents' fiftieth anniversary?" he asked. "Well, now you can get some practice with a grandpa. I have four grandchildren, three boys and a girl."

He danced okay, and I made it through the waltz with him. His fingers felt limp, bony, and dry after Stanley's smooth, warm hands that were firm and strong from metalworking.

"Whew, am I glad to see you!" Stanley exclaimed

41

when the dance was over. "Did you see who I drew? The amazon!"

"How was it?"

"I couldn't lead her. She kept taking over and correcting me, and I got all mixed up. She's got to be six-feet-two in her bare feet, and with those heels, I couldn't even see where I was going. She said her fiancé used to be a pro basketball player. Now he's looking for a coaching job. They hope to make some money entering ballroom-dance contests."

"Do you think they'll make it?" I burst out laughing and the sour expression on Stanley's face smoothed into a smile and he started laughing, too, as we went outside.

"Good luck on the field trip," I said. "It might turn out to be good strategy to miss the tea dance. Daphne will wonder what happened, which will keep her in suspense, and then she'll be worried whether you'll show up at the next party."

Stanley gave me a wide grin.

"Don't let the operator of the Monster Loop put you into orbit," I yelled as he dashed toward the parking lot.

My dad pulled up just then, and after I got in with him, he remarked, "If you have any time after school tomorrow, you might come by the shop and we'll fool around with the invitations to the golden wedding anniversary party. You wanted to help, didn't you?"

My dad runs a print shop and he lets me come in and learn about typesetting and layout. Everything is getting converted to computers, and I have a lot to catch up on.

"Sure," I said. "I could get there by four."

That was how I happened to meet Bob Holloway, who had an after-school job cleaning up the print shop and doing other chores. I watched him wield the push broom against the paper on the floor with graceful, fluid movements.

"Who's that?" I asked my dad.

"Bob Holloway," Dad said. "That shows how long it's been since you paid us a visit. Bob's been doing odd jobs around here for a couple of months." He introduced us.

Bob was terrific-looking, rugged, with an easygoing smile and an open, friendly attitude. While my dad and I were spacing the words on the announcement, Bob came over and watched and made a couple of suggestions. It was then that the idea struck me to add him to my list of candidates for party escort.

I trailed him while he unloaded some reams of paper from cartons and cleaned the glass on one of the copying machines, getting to know him as well as I could, in case I invited him.

I thought about Bob Holloway a lot after I'd left the shop, and I kept inventing excuses to go back to see him during the next week. For instance, I didn't really need my allowance a day early, but that was an excuse to go in and check out Bob.

I planned to announce my third candidate to Stanley at the next dance class. But Stanley got the jump on me and brought up the subject of my escort himself. "I realized that your friend is the Dennis Ridge in my metal-shop class," he said.

"I hope you didn't say anything to him about the anniversary party."

"Of course not. I didn't say anything to him about anything. I happened to remember his name. So when I saw him I checked him out so I can give you more informed advice about your choice."

"So, what did you think?"

"He's okay. He's the gardener, right?"

" 'Okay'? Is that all you can say?"

"I wouldn't want to pass judgment until I'd seen the other guy, Whitehead. He goes to Hillview also?"

"Sure."

"I'll keep an eye out for him, so I'll have some basis for comparison."

This irritated me. "I don't remember hiring you as a private eye," I said.

"No, but you've talked to me about this several times, which makes me think you want my opinion. And I'd like to be able to help you."

I resented Stanley shadowing my acquaintances. Maybe I didn't want him comparing them to Daphne and her glamorous friends. My voice was slightly frosty when I informed him, "It may not be between just those two after all. There's someone else in the picture now. I just met him, and he's sort of interested in this party, so I may invite him."

Before Stanley had a chance to quiz me about the new contender, Mrs. Kriek and Mr. Fancher had called the class to order.

Mr. Fancher made a little speech about the lindy, our new dance for that night. The lindy had been revolutionary in its day, he said, because it was so fast, and the dancers were free to do a lot of their own thing, like in rock.

Then Mrs. Kriek taught us the basics and said we'd learn such variations as the mooch, the sugarfoot walk, and the triple lindy. She put a tape on and we were off. Mr. Fancher made the rounds and prodded us to hold hands correctly so Stanley could swing me away and jerk me back.

The lindy took a lot of energy, so we couldn't talk, and we ended up breathless at the intermission.

"You were saying there's a new guy in the scenario," Stanley said as we sat down. "So tell me about him."

"I don't want to discuss him yet," I said. "As I told you, I just met him."

"Where?"

"Actually he works in my dad's print shop," I said, instantly sorry that I had said it. I had visions of Stanley going down to scout Bob out. "But I've been wondering how your field trip was."

This query succeeded in diverting Stanley from the subject of my date-to-be, and he lit up like the Fourth of July. He bombarded me for the rest of the intermission with statistics on gravitational force, ascending acceleration, drag, momentum, and velocity.

When we were back on the dance floor he surveyed the room and whispered, "I think you and I might be the star pupils."

Stanley was right. We were becoming hotshot dancers. In the lindy we had more energy than the older couples. And we weren't working so hard, so we were having more fun. Stanley had totally relaxed, and so had I.

"You'll do great with Daphne this weekend," I prophesied, swiveling to the left and then to the right. "And don't forget to get interested in the other people at the party so Daphne will see that you can talk to anyone."

"I'll start by practicing on you. Tell me something you've been doing today."

"Not much. Oh, I had duty at the child-care center."

"What child-care center?"

"At school. Some girls who have babies keep them there so they can go to classes and get their diplomas, and some of us from home ec work in there. There's this one baby who's my favorite. Gabriel. Only his mother is a witch. She always makes remarks to me and my friend Thelma. She has a wicked mouth. I only hope she doesn't use it on Gabriel. Poor little fellow, he has no father to stick up for him."

"He's got to have a father," Stanley said.

"Not one that claims him," I said. "Another thing that makes it kind of hard in the child-care center is that we don't have enough room in the nursery. Mrs. Gadsden wishes we had a mobile classroom so it would be kind of separate from the school. She's afraid that when all those babies get out of their cribs and start crawling, we're in for trouble."

Stanley asked a lot of questions, including where the child-care center was and when I was on duty.

"You're a perfect socializer," I complimented him.

"You probably aren't interested in that activity, but you made me think it was vitally important to you."

"But I *was* interested," he insisted. "I never even knew there was anything like that at school. Besides, haven't I always been interested in what you tell me? Like about your escort? I've been thinking, you'd better not wait much longer to pick your partner. You don't have a lot of time to teach him to dance. I've also been thinking that it might not be such a good idea to invite one of your father's employees. So you ought to think that over carefully before you invite— what's his name?"

"Never mind," I said.

Stanley scowled at being denied this information, and I scowled back. He was getting too nosy.

There was a small notice in the paper the next day that Mrs. Schuyler Ridley would be hostess at a dinner dance for her niece Jennifer, one of the current crop of debutantes, on next Saturday evening. I hoped that Stanley would wow Daphne that night. I was concerned about his being an outsider who went to public school. Would he get tongue-tied? Would he be able to avoid stumbling when he was dancing with Daphne? After all, he'd had only four lessons.

But I forgot about Stanley quickly because I had my own problems to worry about. On the Sunday after the Ridley party our whole family went to the annual church picnic, and who should be there but Kent Whitehead?

Stanley was right, I'd better get on the ball. There was Kent. A perfect opportunity to talk to him.

47

So I sidled up to him and said, "How've you been? I haven't seen you since camp." Kent and I had been in a counselors' training program at summer camp and we both hoped to be counselors the next summer. At least we had that in common.

"Okay," Kent replied, looking down at his initials, which he was writing in the dirt with a stick.

"Is your family here?" I asked.

"Over there." He pointed the stick in the direction of a grove.

"Are you going to sign up for the softball game?"

"I guess so."

"So am I. Why don't we go over to the field and see how it's shaping up?"

Kent darted a glance at me as if he were scared of me. "Might as well," he conceded.

I took off for the baseball diamond, with Kent lagging a few steps behind me.

"Hurry up," I prodded, turning impatiently.

"I'm coming."

I waited until he caught up to me. By the time I reached the baseball diamond, he had fallen behind as if he were reluctant to arrive with me. We both signed up, but were on opposite sides. Was that relief I detected on Kent's face? Obviously I made him ill-at-ease. But he'd get used to me once I had issued my invitation.

The baseball teams were composed of all ages— from grandpas to seven-year-olds. Lee Ann, my friend, was out on the sidelines. She wouldn't sign up because her mom was playing.

I was second base on our team. Kent was pitcher on

his. He struck me out on my first time up at bat. If he'd known I was about to invite him to the anniversary party, he'd probably have been easier on me. He didn't look at all remorseful.

But I'm not a type to be discouraged easily. My grandma had told me that sometimes people who seem remote and unfriendly are really only shy and hope you'll make the moves. I wasn't giving up on Kent— yet. But he did require a lot of effort. Later I tried to wedge myself behind him in the food line so I'd be able to follow him to a table.

Kent was just moving past the baked beans when I muscled in. I guess people thought I was with him, because no one objected.

"Your pitching was terrific," I said to him, taking the ladle he was about to replace in the bean pot. "But I finally got a hit off you, even if it was a measly one-base hit."

"We won," he reminded me, moving to a vat of wieners swimming in tomato goop.

"Not by much," I reminded him, despairing of inspiring Kent to anything beyond monosyllabic communication. He just went on filling his plate and acting as if I weren't there.

Kent was not bad-looking. He had regular features, even if his eyes were a kind of a washed-out blue—to match his personality, I thought. His hair was charcoal black, and now was plastered to his scalp because of the baseball cap he'd been wearing. Anyway, he'd be a presentable escort, if dressed up, and I persisted in trying to break down his indifference.

Some other guys called Kent over to a table they

were holding, and I tagged along and grabbed one of the seats. Lee Ann appeared, out-of-sorts.

"Why didn't you wait for me?" she asked. "Save me a place. I'll get a plate."

"This table was for guys only," someone said.

"I don't see any Reserved sign on it," I said, knowing I was intruding, but hoping to get involved in the conversation.

Kent had set his plate down on the opposite side of the table from mine. I definitely wasn't going to get a chance to bring up the subject of the anniversary party now.

5

ON THE WAY HOME from the picnic, I sat between my grandma and grandpa. "I hope to bring a date to the anniversary party," I said, "but I haven't asked anybody yet."

"Maybe you won't have to. I may need a date myself," Grandpa said with a frosty glance at Grandma.

"Oh, Milford, don't be childish about this," Grandma exclaimed. "It's only a five-week trip. I'll be back in time for the anniversary."

"Did you hear that, Meggie? She says *only* and *five weeks* in the same breath. Five weeks is a long time, in case you don't know," Grandpa said.

I shrank back in my seat, realizing that I was caught in the middle of one of my grandparents' arguments, which occurred every time Grandma decided to take off for some faraway, uncharted wilderness with one of her ecology groups. I tried to be inconspicuous, keeping my ears open for clues as to what Grandma was up to.

"Of all the fool schemes! Peru has got to be the most dangerous place they could head for right now," Grandpa said. His eyebrows stood out like projectiles over his fiery black eyes. "There's a bunch of crazed guerrillas tossing bombs around down there like tennis balls. Someone could get hurt."

"But, Milford, you don't understand. We won't be in the cities much. We'll be in the Urubamba Reserve. In this one tiny area of the world there are supposedly more animal species than can be found anyplace else. And scientists are discovering new ones all the time there. Why, I could see some creature that no human being has ever laid eyes on."

"You'll risk your life to look at a bunch of lizards and bugs, when we're right on the eve of our big whing-ding!"

"Risk my life! Do you think revolutionaries are going to be interested in a few tourists out in the boondocks? I was just lucky I heard about this trip, and luckier still that someone dropped out so I could go."

"You told them you'd go without even consulting me." Grandpa sounded aggrieved.

"It never occurred to me that you'd dream of denying me this once-in-a-lifetime opportunity. I'll be back a good four days before the party. And the children are taking care of all the arrangements. There's nothing for me to do here, anyway. And I'll be able to liven up the party with accounts of my Peruvian adventures."

Grandma and Grandpa kept arguing across me, and I remained as invisible as possible. I'd heard these discussions before, and they didn't bother me now. Grandma always went where she wanted to, and they always made up as soon as she got back. Grandma would sometimes lecture about saving the rain forest to some group, and Grandpa would be sitting there, quietly beaming, as if he were the one who organized these expeditions.

"Remember that time you went to the swamp in Brazil?" Grandpa scolded. "I almost had to bring you home from the airport on a stretcher. You were laid up for two weeks afterward. Considering all the work the children are putting into this party, we owe them some assurance that the guests of honor will be there, and will be ambulatory."

Grandma dismissed Grandpa's concerns. "That Brazil trip was years ago," she said. "They have all kinds of new medications and inoculations against tropical diseases now. I'll come back fit as a fiddle. If you had any sense of adventure, you'd be coming along with me; then you wouldn't have to worry."

"You don't have to go halfway around the world to have adventures," Grandpa replied. "I've got activity enough right here to keep me interested."

I knew that Grandpa would be absorbed in his refugee farmers as soon as Grandma got her bags packed and took off. I also knew that my mom and dad and aunts and uncles would go on with their plans for the party, for which I still didn't have a date.

I liked to think that, like Daphne Wainwright, I would be making a kind of debut at my grandparents' party, my first time out with a date. The thought struck me suddenly that maybe none of the three dates I had in mind would accept, and then I'd end up going with my kid brother, Kevin. Some debut!

I decided not to give up on Kent. Maybe he was uncommunicative, but he had his good features. As I said, he was fairly good-looking. He seemed to have quite a few friends among the guys, so his personality couldn't be a total disaster. Maybe I could make him talk, as I'd done with Stanley. I decided to continue to break down his indifference.

I planned to talk the matter over with Stanley at our next ballroom-dancing session. Since he had once been as reserved as Kent, he'd be able to give me some good pointers.

But the minute Stanley plunged through the door of the multipurpose room, I could see he was in no mood to discuss Kent Whitehead—or anything. Obviously he had troubles of his own. His eyebrows were drawn together in the middle so that they slanted down in an expression of distress. His mouth was a tight, straight line. He didn't walk with his jaunty new gait, but with his old stilted shuffle. Furthermore, he didn't even come up to greet me as he had done the last couple of Tuesdays. Instead, he made straight for the water cooler and hung out there until Mrs. Kriek sounded her gong and called for us to get into position.

Stanley gave me a brief unhappy nod when we were together, as if he wanted to become a stranger again.

"We'll start tonight by learning one of the dances originated by our neighbors south of the border," Mrs.

Kriek announced. Stanley emitted a groan and muttered in a bitter voice, *"Now* we learn it."

He faced me with a scowl. Mr. Fancher appeared and adjusted our positions. "Palms down!" He turned our hands and clamped Stanley's to mine. "Shoulders up, head held proudly!" He scrunched back my shoulders and flipped up my chin under Stanley's scrutiny.

Within Stanley's rigid grip I tried to master what Mrs. Kriek called the Cuban motion. *"Very* small steps!" she instructed. "Feet flat. Quick, quick, slow."

Stanley and I woodenly executed the boxy steps, but Stanley wasn't getting the subtle knee bends or transfers of weight. Our rumba was more of a bumble.

"Relax!" I scolded him. "What's the matter with you tonight, anyway?"

Stanley gave me the offended look he had worn at our first meeting, letting me know I had no right to criticize him. He went on jumbling the rumba.

Mr. Fancher came around and clucked his tongue at us. He was stern with Stanley, correcting everything he did.

When the instructor had gone, I said, "Why don't you apply one of your equations to this dance? So much forward velocity, this and that amount of weight transferred to your left hip joint, et cetera."

"The thing is, it's too late." Stanley plowed into the rumba with a little more feeling, and his problem began to gush out. "It turned out that Jennifer Ridley's brother was an exchange student in Latin America last year and they're all freaked-out on South American music. So there wasn't a waltz or fox-trot played at that whole party. Tangos, mambos, bossa novas, rumbas—that's all the combo could play. I didn't have a clue how to dance to that music. There were these guys who were experts in it prancing around with Daphne, while I just hid out on the balcony most of the time."

"Wow, that was a bad break," I said.

Stanley retreated under his black cloud again, remaining perfectly silent while we perfected the square shape of the rumba with our tiny steps.

"I don't know why I even came back." Stanley's voice was choked with frustration. "What's the use of learning this when I've already blown it?"

I felt a touch of panic. What would happen to me if Stanley quit? Would I have to dance with Mr. Fancher? I needed Stanley to finish the course. We still had five lessons after tonight. I racked my brain to think of arguments for him to continue.

"But you've paid your twenty-five dollars," I reasoned. "You don't want to waste that."

Stanley gave me a withering look, and I realized how paltry twenty-five dollars must seem to someone with such a wealthy father.

"Well, hey, you're getting it," I said, encouraging him. "I think your joints are getting oiled up. The next party will be different. You'll move in on Daphne with your expert footwork."

"It'll be my luck that Jennifer Ridley's is the last party where they play Latin music. There was this guy named Sonny Whitlow, whose father had been a foreign-service officer in Argentina, and he was like a pro at these dances. He latched on to Daphne right away.

No wonder! You should see her. She has this sensational curly gold hair that sort of ripples down her back and these incredible dark blue eyes. Once she accidentally made major eye contact with me, and that's when I escaped to the balcony."

"You know what you should have done? You should have gone right up to her and said you didn't know how to do South American dances, but you were dying to dance with her. I'll bet she would have said, 'Come on, I'll teach you.' "

Stanley looked at me condescendingly. "All the other guys would have made fun of me. I would have been the joke of the party, and I wouldn't have been able to show my face at the cotillion."

"You could have told Mrs. Ridley you didn't know how to do those dances. She might have arranged to have some other kind of music played."

"I'm sure the Ridleys would have been happy to change their party plans."

"So you didn't even talk to Daphne? Stanley Stoneman, you are hopeless. I thought you were getting to be social, and now you go to a party where Daphne is and you totally ignore her."

"I had to. I didn't want her to find out what a nondancing, boring person I am."

"You were probably the most *un*-boring person at that party. You have to show Daphne the real Stanley. But now that you've treated her as if she has leprosy, she might just see you as a mystery man. If I were Daphne, and you had been assigned to be my escort, I would be very intrigued now. First, you don't even appear at one party. Then you show up at the next one, but don't pay any attention to her. She has to be fascinated by your aloofness. When the time comes to be her escort at the cotillion, she'll be all keyed-up. You'll be through with the ten ballroom lessons, and those other guys won't have a chance."

"You're just saying that," Stanley said. "You know I'm not the type girls go for." Nevertheless, a slight smile replaced his scowl.

Stanley was going to need a lot of ego building to make it with Daphne, so I thought up a few more things to make him feel good. "Why not?" I asked. "You're good-looking, tall, nice eyes, and nice smile when you loosen up. Good build. The only trouble is you're too inhibited most of the time. You need to loosen up and quit being so self-conscious. Sometimes when you lighten up, you're practically the most attractive guy I've ever seen. Everybody here comments on what a neat person you are."

"Yeah? Who, for instance?" Stanley looked skeptical.

"The Pottses think you're great. Jerrolyn . . . the basketball couple . . ." I was sort of making up some of that to build Stanley's confidence, but it was probably true.

He shrugged. "It's easier to be natural around here where there's nobody who's important. Who cares whether anybody at this class sees me falling all over my own feet? It doesn't matter to you if I twirl you around and we come out back-to-back. In fact, you think it's funny. But I could never get away with doing that to Daphne. I'd be disgraced. Before I even talk to her I want to have my conversation all planned out so

58

she won't stop liking me before she even begins." The worry lines reappeared between Stanley's eyebrows.

"Kent Whitehead seems to have the same problem you have. When I try to talk to Kent, he just clams up. All I get from him is a yes or no."

"I know the feeling," Stanley said. "He probably feels the same way about you as I do about Daphne. Maybe he's desperate to impress you, and he's afraid of saying something stupid, so he figures it's better not to say anything at all."

"I doubt if that's it. At least, he hasn't given any hint of it."

"Daphne doesn't have any hint of how fantastic I think she is, either, because I'm not ready to reveal my true feelings to her."

"But there's a difference in our situations. I don't have those feelings about him that you have about Daphne. I just need somebody to go to Grandma and Grandpa's party with, and I'm not even sure I want it to be him. It might be Dennis, or even Bob."

"You're as bad as Daphne. You have too many guys to choose from, although in many ways you're the complete opposite of her."

I wasn't particularly flattered by that last remark, after he'd just described Daphne's perfection, telling me how dazzling she was. That would make me a drab nonentity. My dark hair was a poor contrast to her shimmering blond mane. I was an ordinary, workaday type, whereas she was a glitzy social butterfly.

I had asked my grandma about being a debutante, and she told me she thought the fathers paid a lot of money to some charity so their daughters could participate in the cotillion. My dad would never go for that.

The triangle sounded and we had to return to the floor to learn some complicated variations of the rumba. It turned out that I had psyched Stanley up enough that he became so skillful at maneuvers like crossing his right foot in back of his left and turning me into promenade position that Mr. Fancher had us give a demonstration of the right way to do it.

"You're the next Fred Astaire," I told Stanley. "None of Daphne's other friends could possibly be better than you."

"It's all a matter of weight, balance, and timing," he said, looking pleased with himself.

In fact, his success with the rumba seemed to get Stanley perked up completely.

He guided me through a maneuver called the wrap-around, where I went clear around him with my arm around his waist. When I reappeared in front of him, he said, "I saw you going into the nurse's office today between second and third periods. I was afraid you were sick or something. Then I remembered what you told me about the nursery for the fatherless babies."

"Right. That's where I was headed. I volunteer there every Tuesday and Thursday during third period. As usual, I had to take my biweekly put-down from Emerald Green, Gabriel's mother. She's bitter, I guess, about being dumped by Gabriel's father, and she has to take it out on someone."

"You're really good at analyzing people," Stanley said. "You ought to be a psychologist someday. But maybe she has a right to be bitter. It burns me up that those fathers aren't more responsible. They run around free as birds when they have kids being cared for by people like you—right where they go to school.''

''Do you think they do? That maybe they're in our classes?''

''It could be.''

''You're right. There's no justice.''

Stanley adroitly stepped to the side, putting gentle pressure on my back in a perfect cross-body lead, and we were involved in a complicated figure that stopped our conversation momentarily.

It was fun to dance with Stanley. I was sorry when the rumba session was over.

6

AT OUR HOUSE the next day there was hysteria about Grandma's trip. She had only a couple of hours left to prepare. Grandpa sulked, and then I heard him gun his pickup truck. It sputtered off down the street. He had Butterfinger, his dog, in the front seat with him for consolation, and I knew he was going to hide out with the refugee farmers while Grandma left. My dad continued to harangue her with news of political unrest in Peru, and my mom raised the subject of gruesome tropical diseases and painful altitude sickness people could suffer in the Andes. Grandma simply flourished a bottle of chloroquine pills and her certificate of a yellow-fever shot and went on packing her safari clothes, hiking boots, and insect repellent.

"If there's anything you desperately want to do in life, Megan, do it," Grandma advised me, holding up a safari jacket with pockets all over it. "Don't wait till you're as old as I am. Why, I shudder to think that I might have missed out completely on seeing the cock-of-the-rock or the resplendent quetzal. Some of these creatures are very rare now, and I wish I might have gone to Peru when they were more plentiful, but better late than never. There's a gold rush in Peru, and also exploration for oil, which is damaging the forests. And they say the natives are coming down the river with chain saws, taking out more of the rain forest."

"What's this?" I asked, picking up a glass tube.

"A water purifier. We'll be in places where the water is polluted, and this will filter it out."

"I just wish you could have planned this trip a few months away from the anniversary party," my dad said. "We're already at the point of no return on our arrangements. The invitations are printed and the food and decorations ordered."

Grandma gave an impatient grimace. "I can't see how this trip will interfere with those plans. I'll be back four days before the party. Now, shoo yourselves out of here and let me get my packing finished. I only have an hour." Grandma was limited to a small amount of luggage and she had to make decisions about what to leave out. Guidebooks and bird books were heavy and bulky, but necessary, as were her film and cameras. Grandma ended up with very little room for her clothing, so she took out her jeans, which she said took too long to dry while traveling. She wore her hiking boots to the plane. Since Grandpa had refused to help her, my dad and I drove her.

"I wish I could go with you," I said. The controversy and Grandma's determination to go made the whole thing seem romantic and exciting to me.

Grandma peered out from under the brim of a turned-down sailor hat. "They don't have any more room on this expedition, Megan, but when you're ready to go, don't let anything stand in your way."

We deposited her and her luggage in the San Francisco airport, where the other members of her group were assembled around an untidy pile of luggage, tripods, and audio equipment. Grandma's eyes glittered with anticipation. She bade us a quick good-bye and turned to her companions, some of whom seemed to be just a little bit older than I am.

"Your grandma is one determined lady," Dad said to me on the way home.

"She sure has lots of energy," I added. "Are you really worried that she won't be back in time for the party, Dad? Because I'm planning to invite a date, and I'd hate to go to all that trouble if the party might not come off."

"Oh, I expect she'll be back, even if she has to hijack a plane. Her airline ticket says she will, anyway. Your mom and I tried to dissuade her for lots of reasons. One, of course, is the date of the party. Another is that your grandma is getting older. She's seventy and still trekking off to out-of-the-way, inaccessible places that are very strenuous for a person her age."

"She doesn't seem old to me. But Grandma is very important to us, and I don't want anything to happen to her."

Mom and Dad seemed reconciled to her trip, however, and so did Grandpa, after a few hours of sulking.

I had quit being concerned about her, too, when I

went to school the next day, and that allowed me to resume worrying about my escort to the anniversary party. That's what I was doing when I reported for duty at the day-care nursery—worrying. I was just replacing Gabriel's pacifier in his mouth when the door was pushed in and who should be there but Stanley Stoneman.

For a moment I was speechless. Then I picked up Gabriel and stood up from the kiddie chair on which I'd been sitting. "Hey, this is the nursery," I exclaimed. "You're not supposed to be in here."

"Why not? I didn't see any sign saying 'No admittance.' I need to talk about something with you."

"Can't it wait till I get out, or till Tuesday night? This has got to be the worst place in school to talk about anything. And guys don't belong in here. What's it about? Your latest bulletin on Daphne, I suppose."

"Well, in general. But why do you say guys can't come in here? Didn't you say yourself that you felt sorry for these babies because they had no fathers? Maybe it would be a good thing if a man came in here to show them there are two kinds of people in the world." Stanley leaned down and stared into Gabriel's face. "Right, fella? You'd like to associate with your own kind, wouldn't you?" He looked over Gabriel's bald head toward me. "That's the type of head people compare to a billiard ball, right?" He laughed.

Gabriel looked at Stanley with eyes as round as plates, and continued to suck on his pacifier.

"This kid is a real clown," Stanley observed. He surveyed the other babies in the cribs. "So this is where you spend your study hall."

"They really need me here," I told him. "When Mrs. Gadsden made her pitch for home-ec students to volunteer to work here a couple of hours a week, not many kids responded, and we still don't have enough people. Mrs. Gadsden had hoped to make this a model for other schools."

"As long as all the kids are quiet, could we talk a bit?"

"Mrs. Gadsden might find you here and she might kick me out of the project for having friends in. Besides, when Thelma gets here, it'll be too crowded."

"Maybe she won't show up, and you can tell Mrs. Gadsden I'm taking her place. I'll give her a spiel about boys needing to be around little kids, too. All the movies and sitcoms now show single dads in charge of babies."

"Okay, until Thelma comes, tell me what your problem is. But be quick." I was uneasy about Stanley being there and wasn't convinced that he was serious about being involved in the day-care nursery.

"See, there's this party tonight at Brenda Clough's. I wondered if you thought I should go right up to Daphne and stake my claim or if you thought I should hang around other people for a while and see if she makes a move on me, you know, pretending to be indifferent, like you said might attract a girl."

"Nobody has dates to this party?"

"It's a free-for-all."

"Talking to some of the others—guys as well as girls—might be best. Talking to her won't be so earth-shattering after you've already loosened up with the others."

"You really think that's the way to go?"

"Of course. It won't hurt to try. Daphne can't do anything drastic like break her date with you to the cotillion, since that's already been printed in the paper."

Stanley absently picked up little Gabriel, who had slithered out of my arms and was about to throw a block at a baby in an Infanseat. "Right. That date is practically written in stone," he agreed, suddenly plopping to the floor and holding Gabriel up over his head. Gabriel gurgled and giggled with delight.

That made me giggle, too, just as an office messenger came in with a note that Thelma would not be in today.

"Did you know she wouldn't be in?" I asked Stanley.

Stanley gave me a lopsided smile. "I confess. I was in the office checking your schedule to make sure you were going to be here, and I heard them say Thelma wouldn't be here. So I rushed down to take her place."

"You're a lot bigger than Thelma. You take up much more room. See how cramped it is in here? You really didn't intend to help out, did you?"

"Of course. Why not?"

"You ever been around babies?"

"No." Stanley glanced around at the four cribs, where two of the babies were sleeping. One had captured his toes and was looking startled by such curious objects.

"This doesn't look like too hard a job, except for keeping this wiggly weirdo under control." Stanley grabbed Gabriel again.

"I can't believe you're in here doing this. It's hysterical." I had to stifle one of my fits of uncontrollable laughter to keep from waking up the two babies.

Stanley's face became serious. "I really came here for selfish reasons. It was just that I was worrying about how to act at the party, and you're the only person I've ever talked to about this kind of problem. I get so emotional about it, and you're such an unbiased listener."

"A sounding board, right?" I said in a flat voice.

"Right. You don't mind, do you, since the party's tonight. Obviously I couldn't wait till I saw you on Tuesday, and I thought, well, she's right here. . . . It was urgent for me to get insight from a girl on Daphne's probable reaction to me before I did something dumb at the party."

Gabriel squirmed out of Stanley's grasp and crawled rapidly across the room toward the baby in the Infanseat. Stanley made a dive, capturing him before he could terrorize the smaller infant.

"I don't have any aspirations to run an advice-to-the-lovelorn service." I tried to sound cold and indifferent. Frankly, I was becoming a little resentful about Daphne.

"You're practically the only girl I know. All the other girls I come across tune out when I turn up. And it takes a girl to know a girl, right? So where else could I go to get advice on how to proceed with Daphne except to you? Your advice is really important, especially now, when I'm about to come face-to-face—to quote a corny cliché—with the girl of my dreams."

It ticked me off suddenly to have Stanley break into

my duty at the day-care nursery to get maudlin over Daphne. It wasn't the right place. It made me feel angry. But I bit my tongue.

"And she's the girl of a few other guys' dreams, too, right? I can't give you very good advice when I don't know any of these others."

"They're a fairly homogeneous mass. They all go to private schools. I'm the only one who goes to a public school." He said this while still holding Gabriel, who was looking sleepy now.

"That helps to make you stand out by being different. You might get Daphne's interest by letting her know you're rugged and can hold your own with the kids in public school. How about telling her about this day nursery? They don't have anything like this at those academies. Tell her you're going in for public service and improving the world. You're promoting this nursery so fatherless infants can have a better life." I took the sleeping Gabriel from Stanley and put him down.

Stanley listened alertly. "That just might be a good topic. My mother, who once was a debutante herself, says that all the debutantes have to do some charity work. I think Daphne has to work an hour a week at a secondhand shop where they sell their used clothes and other things. But she probably hasn't ever been near a day-care nursery."

I had that feeling wash over me again of wishing I never had to listen to another word about Daphne Wainwright.

A disturbance came from one of the cribs. The baby in it had screwed up her face and I could see a howl would soon be emerging. I turned her over. She gave a big burp and then threw up, and that ended our discussion of Daphne.

"I'd better go now," Stanley said.

"How about helping me clean this up?" I suggested, just as the school nurse stuck her head in the door. She gave a start when she saw Stanley.

"What's going on in here?" she asked, frowning.

"Thelma sent word that she wouldn't be in, and Stanley is filling in for her."

"Are you from home ec?" the nurse asked.

"No, metal shop." Stanley's face turned ruddy. He looked uncomfortable. I handed him the baby, after wiping it off, so I could change the crib sheets.

"This is very irregular," the nurse said.

"It was an emergency," I said, bustling around to illustrate my point. "And Stanley thought that since these babies have no fathers, it might be good to let them see a boy for a change."

The nurse viewed him suspiciously and looked at her watch.

"You can finish out the hour," she said to Stanley, "but in the future, we'll have only registered attendants. Visits from their boyfriends are not allowed." The nurse retreated into her office.

"Looks like I got you in hot water," Stanley commented.

"And yourself, too."

"Well, anyway, I'm sorry I barged in like this." Stanley held the baby as if it were a time bomb.

"Let's see," I said, "which baby is that? Turn it around." Stanley held it with his hand on its back, but

70

a few inches away from him, as if he were going to do the fox-trot with it. I couldn't help laughing. "Put it in promenade position," I ordered.

When he pivoted the baby, I could see that it was Melissa, whose mother was a tiny, delicate Asian refugee. Of all the mothers, she was probably the most conscientious and the most determined to finish high school. In contrast to Emerald, she always expressed her gratitude for help in caring for her three-month-old.

I located Melissa's tote bag and found a change of clothing, took her from Stanley, and changed her from the skin out. "Now you've had a demonstration. You have to do the next one all by yourself," I said, teasing him.

"I'm outta here!" Stanley exclaimed.

"No, you don't." I put the baby back in the crib and she went to sleep.

"I never thought of the consequences when I came in. Did you notice how the nurse seemed to suspect me of something? What if she, or anybody else, for that matter, thought I was—you know—involved with one of these kids?"

That made me hysterical again. "Stanley Stoneman, you are the worst worrywart I ever knew," I said.

"They *could* think that," he insisted. "You said yourself it was highly unusual for a guy to come in here. So that nurse probably thought I wouldn't be here unless I had an ulterior motive—some special reason for wanting to see one of these babies."

"It's too bad one of those irresponsible fathers doesn't drop in here once in a while," I said. "They

71

ought to be required to share in helping out with their own babies.''

''They're probably scared stiff that somebody will find out who they are,'' Stanley said, looking soberly across the crib.

All the babies were quiet now. I hoped Stanley wouldn't dump anything more on me about the delectable Daphne. When he started to revive the subject, I squelched him.

''Could we drop the subject now? I think I've run out of advice.''

''See, I'm even boring you. So it's fairly certain I'll bore Daphne.''

Stanley looked like a hurt little boy, and despite the phantom of Daphne hovering over him, I felt like seizing him in our waltz grip, but the possibility of the nurse popping in again inhibited me.

''Incidentally,'' Stanley continued, ''maybe I told you Dennis Ridge is in my metal-shop class.''

''You mentioned it a while back.''

''I've been keeping an eye on him, in case you ask for any further advice about him.''

''And do you have anything to say about him?''

''The only thing that might be of interest to you is that he's not too well-coordinated. While I watched him yesterday, he trashed two sheets of metal. The first one slipped out of the saw and got mangled, and he did the identical thing with the second. But our teacher stopped him before he wrecked the saw.''

''Grandpa never complained about his letting the lawn mower run amok or anything.''

''What I'm saying is that somebody that careless

might not turn out to be a very competent dancing partner.''

"So you think I should cross him off my list?''

"I wouldn't put him at the top of it. You'd have a tough time teaching him to dance, because that's what you're planning, isn't it?''

"That's what I have in mind. But you don't know that the anniversary party itself is in jeopardy, do you?'' I told him about Grandma's trip to the Andes and the Amazon basin in Peru. "She won't be back till four days before the party,'' I said. "And Grandpa is pretty upset. He's afraid she'll miss a connection somewhere and won't get back in time.''

Stanley whistled. "You couldn't have the party without the guest of honor, could you?''

The bell for the end of the period rang and I started to collect my possessions. Emerald Green dropped in to check on Gabriel, and both Stanley and I were the recipients of one of her poisonous glares.

"I see you bring your own entertainment here so you won't have to spend too much time with the babies.'' She gave me an acid look and Stanley a slow, scornful stare.

"Who was that?'' Stanley asked when we were out in the hall.

"Emerald Green, Gabriel's mother. Well, good luck at the party. Hope you make a big hit with Daphne. See you Tuesday.''

I WAS AT DAD'S PRINT SHOP when the invitations came off the press. There were two hundred of them. Bob Holloway put them in boxes after they came out of the folding machine. Fifty invitations and fifty envelopes in each of four boxes.

"Your grandparents must have a lot of friends," Bob said, clamping down the lid on the last box.

"They've been accumulating them for seventy years," I said.

Dad took a look at the sample invitation Bob had kept out for him.

"Looks great," he said to Bob, and then turned to me. "Megan has her work cut out for her, addressing these envelopes."

"I learned calligraphy in a summer recreation course," I told Bob. "I'll print them out with my italic pen."

"Great," he said.

"I wish I could use just a few of these for my friends, Lee Ann and maybe Thelma."

"Absolutely not," Dad said. "This is your grandparents' party, and we've already eliminated a few of their friends we wanted to ask."

"But I get to invite an escort," I informed him. "Grandma already said I could." I glanced at Bob to see if he had any reaction to this news, but he didn't seem to take it personally.

Dad was called to the phone just then, so I had some privacy. I said to Bob, "You should meet my grandparents."

"I hear they're really something."

"After all your work getting out the invitations, you ought to come to the party," I continued.

Bob gave an embarrassed laugh. "Setting up the type only took a few minutes, and running it off not much longer," he said.

Bob was a very appealing guy. He had mahogany-colored curly hair, and some of the curls tumbled down on his forehead. He had a smudge of ink beside the cleft in his chin, and he wore an inky apron tied loosely over his stone-washed jeans.

"I've got to check this printer," he said, turning from me. He stepped across the room to a machine that was spewing out copies of an annual report for some company. He moved sinuously. He'd make a great rumba dancer.

I don't know why I compounded my humiliation by hanging around and wending my way to his side of the room, where he was packaging the annual reports.

"Did you ever take ballroom dancing?" I asked him.

He looked up from his task and gave me a strained, wary smile.

I had just opened my mouth, ready to tell him I was taking a class in ballroom dancing and was in a position to teach him if he'd be my escort for the anniversary party, when Dad barged in. He dumped some work on Bob that sent him to another part of the print shop.

"You'd better take these invitations home now, Megan. It's busy and we need to get them out of the way," Dad told me. Obviously I wasn't going to get another crack at Bob that afternoon. So I stacked up the boxes of invitations and trudged home with them.

I'm very meticulous about my calligraphy, and most of my time over the weekend was taken up with the job of lettering each invitation. Then it was Tuesday again, and I waited at the multipurpose room, debating whether or not to tell Stanley about Bob Holloway.

Stanley practically jogged into the multipurpose room, his head held up, all his worry lines erased, looking like someone who'd just hit a home run or received an A+ on a test. I could tell Stanley was bristling with good news.

"You were right!" He bestowed an approving grin on me. "I was an enigma to Daphne. So I didn't have to approach her at all. I had no sooner walked into that party than I saw Daphne and a couple of her girlfriends whispering together and looking my way. Then they all giggled and pushed Daphne, and she started toward me. Just then this little dog came over and nipped at my ankles and I pretended to be distracted by it. You know, 'Nice doggie, what sharp teeth you have,' so Daphne wouldn't see how excited I was that she was coming my way.

"So I casually looked at her, and before I said anything, she said, 'You're the elusive Stanley Stoneman.' Can you believe it, just the way you predicted.

"I played it cool. 'I don't think so. I've never found myself elusive,' I said.

"She had this fantastic laugh, you know, kind of a trill that twirled around me and grabbed me. She said, 'I'm Daphne Wainwright. You and I are paired up for the cotillion.'

" 'Oh, I've been wanting to meet you,' I said. 'I'm looking forward to the big event.' "

"See, Stanley, after all your worrying, you were on the right track all along."

"Then Daphne was all over me with questions. Why did I go to school where I did; what kind of music did I like; did I have any brothers or sisters, cousins or aunts? Close up, she looks even more terrific than from a distance."

"Did you show her what a skilled dancer you are?"

"No, because there wasn't any dancing at this party. It was only a reception, where people stand around and eat and talk and you can hardly hear yourself think. Various guys, especially this pushy Sonny Whitlow, would come up and try to horn in on our conversation, but Daphne seemed to want to be alone with me. At one point she suggested that we go out in the garden where it wasn't so noisy, but this guy Franklin Houtzkeller followed us out and kept

77

muscling in, bragging about this and that. You know the type.

"I didn't want to hang around, so I made some excuse and took off, and Daphne looked pretty miffed at Franklin. As I was leaving, I could have sworn I heard them arguing."

"So you made definite points with Daphne," I said, not feeling quite as happy for him as I should have.

"Yeah, I guess. She sure knows who I am now."

"I wish I could get my social life as well-organized as yours is," I said. "But mine's still in limbo." I felt slightly depressed to think of Stanley's glittering social events, compared with my tacky trailing of an errand boy around the print shop.

"You still can't get Whitehead to talk?" Stanley asked. He had a way of bending toward me with a concerned air that made me feel momentarily important.

"It's not so much him as Bob Holloway."

"Holloway! The gardener?"

"No, stupid. The gardener is Dennis. Remember, he's in your metal shop. Bob is the one who works in my dad's print shop."

"Your affairs are so confusing. There are so many guys involved that I can't keep them straight."

The triangle sounded and Stanley groaned. "You know what tonight is? The tango. Mr. Fancher warned us last week that it's a real bear. I think it got its name from tangled feet."

"It ought to be a challenge."

"Maybe." Stanley wasn't convinced.

Mr. Fancher gave a speech about the tango, and we went through the steps.

"This is a close-contact dance," Mr. Fancher explained. "In the tango, we eliminate the six inches of daylight that has separated you in the dances we've learned up to now. Gentlemen, extend your arm farther around your partner. Hold her close to you. No daylight showing."

"The tango was called in Spanish the *baile con corte,* 'the dance with a stop,' " Mrs. Kriek added. "Everybody, flex your knees."

Stanley's arm moved farther around me until I was tight against him. It gave me a tingly, warm feeling. I could feel his breath against my hair.

"I'll bet you can hardly wait to tango with Daphne," I said.

Stanley scowled. "That first party I went to, when I hadn't learned the tango, she was doing it with Sonny Whitlow, who had once been to Argentina."

"You'll be better than he is, once you've learned it."

Mr. Fancher and Mrs. Kriek got together and demonstrated a step they called the draw, where one foot is drawn slowly across to the other. Then we had to imitate them.

"Now the corte," Mrs. Kriek announced, and they showed us a step where we stopped to change direction. Last was the fan. We turned on one foot while holding the other behind it.

"This is where I turn up with a few extra left feet," Stanley predicted. His prophecy came true, and we ended up entangled, requiring extra attention from Mrs. Kriek.

"Don't be discouraged," I said, my breath curling around Stanley's ear, which was disturbingly close to my mouth. "We're not the worst, by any means."

The Caribbean-cruise couple were in dire straits, and even the pair who hoped to be exhibition dancers had a long way to go to realize their dream.

Jerrolyn and her beanpole partner had to be taken on separately by Mrs. Kriek and Mr. Fancher.

By intermission Stanley and I had a fair grasp of the dance. "We made a lot of progress." Stanley's voice held a hint of triumph.

Separating from the close contact with Stanley, I felt again that irritating twinge of resentment toward Daphne Wainwright. It felt good to be held by Stanley. He was substantial and steady, and a pleasant warmth had built up between us.

"I was about to tell you my experience with Bob Holloway," I said.

"Oh, I forgot to tell you," he interrupted. "Daphne asked me if I played tennis. I said no, and she said if I wanted to come over to her house sometime, she'd give me some pointers. Do you think I should go?"

"Well, of course you should."

"But she didn't say when."

"You're the one who should say that, stupid!" My irritation was beginning to show. I no longer wanted to be supportive of his courtship of Daphne. I hoped my advice and ego building would go sour. "You really want my opinion?"

"I'm asking for it, aren't I?"

"I think you made your first mistake when you walked off and left Daphne with this Frank Whatcha-makeller. You were making it with her, and it was up to you to tell Frank to buzz off. Second, Daphne was practically asking you to make a date with her. When she offered to teach you tennis, she expected you to leap in and pin down a day and time."

Stanley looked glum. "There's a saying that opportunity knocks only once. Do you think it'll ruin my chances that I didn't pick up on her tennis invitation? She still has to go to the cotillion with me, but that could be very uncomfortable if we don't get along."

There was a clang from the triangle. Now I had made him feel worthless again. I felt sorry for him and decided to build him up anyway. "You have got to quit being so negative about yourself, Stanley. You shouldn't let anybody get in the way of what you want."

I was startled to hear my grandma talking through me—the sum of generations that had gone before me expressing themselves in my advice to Stanley. "I keep telling you, you have everything. Good looks, intelligence, coordination, personality. Only you don't have enough confidence to let those things show."

Stanley reacted to my compliments with grateful surprise. He seized me in the tango grip. We fit to-gether and I snuggled comfortably into his embrace. Wait till Daphne gets the wonderful feel of his holding her, I thought. She'll be his forever.

Then I had to start thinking about the tango, because it was not only complicated but also fun. Mrs. Kriek inserted a tape of "Hernando's Hideaway," and

Mr. Fancher showed us how we could achieve a stealthy look with the stop step, maintaining slow foot movements to the ultimate moment, when the music forced us to move on. Stanley and I pretended to be cat burglars and pickpockets and were so caught up in the hilarity of it that we moved too fast and collided with Mr. and Mrs. Potts.

Mrs. Kriek told us to simmer down.

"Place your foot in back of you, but don't turn your body." She held Stanley's shoulders, demonstrating where his foot should be. "To the side on your left foot. Now, draw left to right foot. Slowly, slowly. Don't transfer your weight. Let's go through that again."

I told Stanley the tango was my favorite dance. Eventually we had everything in order and Mr. Fancher said we looked absolutely elegant on our last run through a number called "Jealousy."

Stanley bowed to me with a big Cheshire-cat grin on his face and said, "Thank you for the dance, senorita."

When we were leaving, he asked me, "How do you get home?"

"Either my dad or my grandpa picks me up," I said. After I climbed into the car beside Grandpa, I wondered if that question had been Stanley's way of asking me if he could give me a ride home. Why else would he ask? Stanley and I were getting to be really good friends, but it would be all over soon. He'd be off to the cotillion and I to the anniversary party with our respective partners. That gave me a bleak feeling.

"Your grandma called tonight," Grandpa said.

"I wish she had called when I was there," I said.

"She's after hummingbirds," he said. "Right out in the hotel garden she spotted five species when she hadn't been there an hour. Remarkable perception, your grandma. She was headed up into the high country. Says some of their party are down with altitude sickness, but not your grandma. That woman is indestructible."

"I hope I'll be like her, Grandpa," I said.

"You are, Meggie. The image of her when she was your age. Always on the go, never daunted by anything. How's the Japanese brush painting going?"

"Great," I said. I had almost forgotten my lie. "Maybe I can ask the teacher how to paint a hummingbird and give it to Grandma as an anniversary present when she gets back."

"*When* she gets back? You mean *if* she gets back." Grandpa gripped the wheel a little tighter. "I get angry all over again to think of what a close shave it will be between your grandma's return flight and that party."

"But, Grandpa, you just said everything was going okay."

"Anything can happen between now and then. Just tonight I read about some revolutionaries tossing a bomb into the lobby of the Bolivar Hotel in Lima, where Lavinia stays the night before she takes off for home."

"But, Grandpa, they say lightning never strikes twice in the same place."

"Well, she can still miss her plane. Why, something could even happen to that canoe she's going to travel in."

83

"Grandpa, you're just manufacturing worries."

"I always figure if I'm prepared for the worst, I'll never be devastated, and if it doesn't happen, I'll be pleasantly surprised."

"But, Grandpa, in the meantime, you're saddling yourself with unnecessary worry."

"Where does a teenage girl get off giving advice to her old grandpa?"

I thought back. True, I had been dispensing advice all evening. First, to Stanley, on how to conduct himself with the glamorous Daphne. Now to my grandpa on his attitude toward his adventurous wife. How could my advice be any good? I had never even had a date, and I was telling Stanley how to be a great date for an outstanding beauty. Why did he even listen to me?

"I guess people never stop having problems, no matter how old they get," I said.

"Right," Grandpa said. He let me out at his driveway, which is right next to ours.

"You might not have to pick me up at the class next week," I said. "I might get a ride home with a friend."

"It seems to me all the class is much older than you," Grandpa said. "I saw them coming out, and some of them were my vintage. They're a strange crowd of brush painters."

"There's one other teenager," I told him.

"Oh, so maybe there's a romance brewing?" Grandpa gave me a twinkly, teasing look.

"Grandpa!" I scolded. "Nothing like that. We just happened to be in the class together. He already has a girlfriend. The reason he came to the class was so he could"—I started to say "learn to dance for her," but I changed it—"impress her with his talent.

"By the way," I added, "do you have anything I could help you with while Grandma's gone? Yardwork? Housework?"

"Yardwork is all taken care of. Dennis will be coming over on Saturday. But how do you feel about washing windows?"

"Terrible, but for you I'll do it."

"Well, show up then, if you're still feeling energetic."

Washing windows, I'd have a really good chance to get acquainted with Dennis Ridge, and maybe this would be the weekend I'd nail down a date for the anniversary party. Then I could forget about Bob Holloway and Kent Whitehead, and at the dance class on Tuesday I'd be able to announce to Stanley that despite his opinion of Dennis, my choice was made.

8

I GOT TO Grandpa's house on Saturday before Dennis did. Grandpa was about to go grocery shopping, but he found me a bucket and sponge and some ammonia and vinegar and the stepladder.

"The house is unlocked, so you can get in," he said.

The living-room windows had lots of small panes that wound out with a crank and were hard to do. The corners never seemed to get clean. I was just finishing a set of eight of these windows when Dennis drove up in an old Ford Falcon that had rusty patches. A statue of a curvy woman was affixed by a suction cup to the dashboard, and it wiggled when the car moved.

Dennis didn't see me at first. He went right to the garage and took out the lawn mower, rake, and push broom. After he had revved up the lawn-mower engine and begun to cut a swath across the front lawn, he stopped short. "Whoa!" he said. "Who's this?"

I was standing outside on the ladder in my shorts, and he looked me over so thoroughly it was embarrassing. I'm sure it didn't take that long to see what skinny legs I had.

"Don't let me interrupt," I said. "I'm just doing the windows for Grandpa."

"You could interrupt me anytime," he said, looking me up and down, pausing at strategic points. "You must be Megan, the Royces' granddaughter. You go to Hillview, right? I saw you in the halls."

"You got it," I said. "These are all done. I guess I'll go inside." I was eager to get away from Dennis' scrutiny.

"Where's your grandpa?"

"Went out to do some shopping."

Dennis had cut the lawn-mower engine, and I didn't hear him starting up again when I descended the ladder and picked up my bucket to go inside.

"Here, let me carry that for you," Dennis said.

"You don't need to," I insisted as he took the bucket from me, touching my arm as he did so. "Grandpa probably wants you to get on with the yardwork."

Dennis seemed to have more than the usual number of hands. He twisted the doorknob and pushed the door in while guiding me with a hand on my waist.

"There, you're in," he said, setting the bucket down by the window. Then he gave me that look again. I knew it couldn't be that he was overwhelmed by my looks. I'm only what you might call a pleasantly wholesome person, and I've heard various relatives say, with a hint of disparagement, "Oh, she has that wide Quinn mouth." (Quinn was my mom's maiden name.) The reference to my mouth seems to refer both to its appearance and to its incessant use, since I have a reputation for being gabby.

"So you're Megan," he said, not moving.

"Uh-huh. I live right next door."

He wouldn't take his eyes off me, and I felt squirmy under his steady gaze. I needed to escape.

It was the perfect chance to say, "If you like looking at me so much, maybe you'd like to be my escort at my grandparents' anniversary party next month." Then the matter would be finished. But the words wouldn't come. Dennis's bold approach caused me to hold back. I had the feeling he might turn out to be one of those guys you had to constantly fight off. I'd heard other girls talking about them.

So I let this chance to get a date for the anniversary party pass by, and I just said in a prissy tone, "We'd better get back to work. Grandpa will be getting back from the store anytime."

"Yeah, I guess," Dennis said. "Let me know when you have to haul that bucket outside again, and I'll be here on the double." He had a nice smile. Maybe I was misinterpreting his moves. I didn't have any experience around boys. It could be that he wasn't coming on to me at all, but was just the helpful conscientious person my grandparents had said he was.

As I cleaned the inside of the windows, I saw him look at me once in a while and I became convinced that he was only an ordinary friendly type. I wasn't accustomed to that. I thought of Stanley Stoneman's haughty reserve when we had first met, Kent White-head's awkward silences, and Bob Holloway's preoc-cupation with his job. Dennis was the only one who seemed really attracted to me, and so he was the logical choice to be my escort.

When I had finished the inside of that one window, I cranked open a side of it and told him I was going to move back out, and he rushed in to carry out the bucket, giving me a kind of possessive look as he did.

"Make sure that ladder's steady," he said when I was up on it. "I better check. Wouldn't want you taking a tumble." He made a gesture at steadying the ladder, his hand grazing my bare leg as he did. My apprehensions about him returned, although he did return quickly to his yardwork.

I became super self-conscious when I was washing the next window, because I could see Dennis glance over at me. He was trimming the borders with the grass clippers now, crawling along the sides of the lawn, looking up about every third clip. I should have worn my jeans instead of my short shorts. I began to hope for Grandpa to get back so I wouldn't be alone with Dennis. But after all, I was right next door to my house. My mom and dad liked to sleep in on Saturday mornings, but Dennis wouldn't get fresh with me if he thought my parents might look out the window. He could always come in when I was doing the insides of the windows, though.

When I went in, however, he didn't follow, and I chided myself for having an overactive imagination. I peeked at him out the window. He was what you'd call stocky. Not fat, but solidly built, sturdy and strong-looking, only about an inch taller than I. Our heads would be practically together if we were dancing. I wouldn't be just barely peeking over his shoulder, as I did over Stanley's. He moved more ponderously than Stanley, who was, basically, a graceful guy.

Would Dennis want to learn ballroom dancing? The thought had probably not occurred to him. I pictured him doing disastrous things to pieces of metal in the shop at school.

When I was on the back porch doing the kitchen windows, Dennis came around with his pruning shears to tidy up the shrubbery, and I decided I'd never have that good a chance to get a date for the anniversary party.

I burst out, "Have you ever done any ballroom dancing?"

Dennis whirled around, startled. "Have I done *what?*"

"You know, waltzes, fox-trots, all that."

His eyes narrowed, and he regarded me suspiciously. "Why?"

Grandpa chose that moment to pull into the drive. The car door burst open and Grandpa asked Dennis to carry some bags of fertilizer out of the trunk, so I remained in an awkward position and Dennis was left bewildered.

Then Grandpa bustled about supervising Dennis at digging out some exhausted marigolds and fertilizing the flowerbeds. I finished the windows, and then, because Dennis and Grandpa were so absorbed in their work, I walked by and said, "The windows are all done, Grandpa. I'm leaving."

"Thanks a million, honey," Grandpa said. Dennis looked up with a puzzled expression and didn't say anything.

When I described this exchange to Stanley at the next session of ballroom dancing, he pounced on me.

"You did the same thing you accused me of doing. You know how you complained that I didn't follow up on Daphne's invitation to play tennis?"

"Yes, and I was right. Since you didn't take her up on it right away, you should phone her and tell her you want to accept her offer to teach you tennis. You can only blame yourself if you let her other boyfriends take over."

"Take your own advice, then. Just be direct. If you insist on having that klutz for your escort, go back to your grandpa's next Saturday and say to him, 'I never got to finish what I was asking you last week. Grandpa and Grandma are having an anniversary party and I thought you might like to go. If you don't know ballroom dancing, I'll teach you.' It's that simple. Although I predict it won't be that simple to teach him to dance."

"Asking him may seem simple to you. But I don't know Dennis that well."

"You never will, unless you make a move."

Mrs. Kriek announced that our tango needed some work. We were going to smooth it out during the first hour, and in the last hour we'd be introduced to the polka.

"Then for the remainder of the course, we're going to review the dances until you're confident about performing them in public. Of course, there are other dances we haven't touched on: the samba, the bossa nova, the merengue, the hustle. Those of you who want to go on into the advanced class can continue adding these dances to your repertoire."

"I'm glad we're going back over those others. I've practically forgotten how to waltz," Stanley said. "The waltz is the most important dance in the cotillion. My mother briefed me on the procedure. First, the escorts make two lines and the debutantes walk between them and through an arch of flowers. At the other side of the arch, their fathers are waiting to dance the first waltz with their daughters. Then I'll get the next dance, which is also a waltz. All the guests will be watching those first waltzes, which are only for the debutantes, the fathers, and the escorts. After that, everyone can come out on the floor."

It depressed me to think of Stanley dancing with someone who had just passed under an arch of flowers, but I soon forgot it, because Stanley and I had fun with the tango. He hammed it up, swooping me back in deep dips.

"Maybe you and I could do a dance at Talent Day in school," he said with a wicked grin.

Mr. Fancher came by and told us to cool it. "It's all very well to improvise," he scolded, "as long as we don't get in the other dancers' way, and I'm afraid you two are distracting the others."

We did a more sedate tango then, and before we learned the polka, Stanley told me all about another science project during our intermission. "NASA has asked high-school students to contribute ideas for a gizmo that can navigate on Mars," he said. "The project is called the Technology Challenge. This gadget has to maneuver over all kinds of obstacles and still keep going. It's keeping me awake nights."

Stanley went on to tell me about how he had to adapt what was known about the Martian atmosphere to the laws of inertia and gravity and apply them to a vehicle that had stumped space engineers.

"I'm working on a design, which I've partially built. Even if it doesn't get to Mars, it'll be featured in the Science Fair. Mr. Grayson says I have a solid scientific basis for my invention. I'm making the component parts in metal shop and assembling them at home in one of our old barns. I'll show it to you sometime if you want."

"You've whetted my curiosity. I'd be interested to see it, even though I'm not planning a trip to Mars anytime soon."

Stanley laughed.

"I guess your new project will prevent you from carrying out your threat to provide a masculine presence in the day-care center."

Stanley wrinkled up his nose. "Speaking of the day-care center, you know what?" His face illuminated with a sudden thought.

"What?"

"Remember that Emerald somebody, the one who's so hostile."

"I wish I could forget her."

"Since you advised me to be more social, I have

gotten more chummy with the guys in metal shop. And yesterday some of them were kidding this George Berglund about how he used to go with some girl named Emerald. There couldn't be another person with that name, could there? George is this big hefty junior. You know, football tackle. He was all over those guys, reacted like a wild man. Mr. Grayson had to break them up and put Berglund on detention."

"It's got to be the same Emerald. There aren't many of those around."

"That's what I thought. You have to make the connection. So I couldn't help linking him with Gabriel too. I took a close look at George, and there's a definite resemblance. Round face, round eyes, only George has hair."

I laughed, but I was somewhat disturbed. What would happen if Stanley had found the father of one of our day-care babies? I decided that if Stanley pursued his investigation, Emerald would be even angrier than she already was.

I had told Grandpa not to come for me that night, thinking that Stanley would ask me if I needed a ride. He failed to do so, however.

I trailed him out to the parking lot and saw him jump in a car that was by no means the Rolls-Royce I had envisioned. It was a weird jalopy that he might have made himself in metal shop. Staney was a constant surprise. I hoped he wasn't planning to pick up Daphne in that car to take her to the cotillion.

Jim and Betty Potts were just getting into their car when I turned around.

Mr. Potts asked me if there was a problem.

"I thought I had a ride home and I don't."

"Come on in, we can take you home," Mrs. Potts offered. When I was in the car, she said, "You and your young man haven't had a tiff, I hope."

"Nothing like that," I said. "He thought my grandpa was coming to pick me up."

All the way home they kept telling me what a nice young man Mr. Linton was. I didn't see any point in enlightening them to the fact that he was neither my young man nor Mr. Linton. After all, in a few weeks we'd all be history to one another. Including Stanley and me. Stanley would be off to the cotillion and I to the anniversary party—with Dennis Ridge? I wasn't sure, and I thought back to my incomplete encounter with Bob Holloway. I ought to take another crack at him.

I told Mr. and Mrs. Potts about my grandma being in South America and rattled on for the rest of the way home. It turned out the Pottses were going in my direction anyway, and they offered me a ride anytime I needed one.

I told them I'd let them know. Actually, I hoped to ride with Stanley next week. There just wasn't enough time to talk on the dance floor. The extra talking time we'd have on the way home would be a real bonus, especially since I needed advice on my situation, which kept getting more and more confused.

In my mind I had practically settled on Dennis Ridge as an escort. Hadn't he stared at me all the time I was washing windows? Maybe he had been *too* interested, but surely he would stay in line at my grandparents' anniversary party. He wouldn't dare make any moves on me right under Grandpa's nose, when Grandpa was part of his source of income.

I had my own income to think of, incidentally, which directed me to my dad's shop to collect my allowance the next afternoon, and in the process, I made another contact with Bob Holloway, who was sealing up some boxes of pamphlets and taking them out to load into Dad's pickup for delivery to the customer.

As you have probably noticed, I'm not the kind of person you'd call shy, and I can be very direct when I put my mind to it. So I just went right up to Bob Holloway back in the storeroom where my dad couldn't scowl at me for distracting the help.

"I guess you must have wondered when I was here last why I should ask you that weird question—you know, whether you had ever taken ballroom dancing."

Bob gave me a look as if I didn't have my head screwed on right. "Oh, yeah," he said, as if he had forgotten the episode. "That is a question one isn't often asked."

He had a patronizing tone, and I was struck by how handsome he was. He had a strong, long face with a square chin that just now was set, as if to tolerate me no matter what I said next.

"If you're still interested in an answer, my parents put me in a dancing class when I was in junior high, and I had fortunately forgotten all about it until you brought up the subject."

As he spoke, I realized how much older he was than Kent Whitehead or Dennis Ridge.

'You don't go to Hillview High, do you?"

"Hardly," he said, again with condescension. "I'm in my second year of junior college."

At least three years older than I. Probably had a flock of girlfriends. But I'm a person who finishes what I start, so I plunged on.

"The reason I asked you was, since you had done all the work on the invitation to my grandparents' anniversary party, you deserved to come to it. Of course, they'll be doing ballroom dancing, so if you come, you ought to know how."

Bob started to laugh and to look at me incredulously. Dad passed by the door.

"Is Megan bothering you?" Dad said with his darkest scowl. "Megan, Bob is working on a rush job. These pamphlets were promised at the client's by four o'clock, and you're holding him up."

"It's under control, Mr. Royce," Bob assured him, taking a stack of boxes out to the alley. When the lot of them were stacked aboard a truck, he jumped in the cab and took off down the alley without giving me the courtesy of a reply.

"Megan!" I knew Dad was going to chew me out. "I'll have to ask you to stay away from the shop if you're coming here to flirt with the employees."

"Sorry, Dad," I said. "What I came for was that I need some new tennis shoes and I had to get my allowance a day early."

I was in a pickle now. Had I asked Bob to be my escort or not? I tried to remember my exact words and to analyze whether they had really constituted an invitation. Bob had been anything but receptive, but had he turned me down—if I had asked him?

The dilemma grew more complicated when I headed for the shoe store, and in front of Jerry and Gary's ice-cream store I ran into Kent Whitehead.

He gave a gulp when he saw me, and then, as if it was a tremendous effort, he said in an unnatural voice, "I was just going in to get an ice-cream cone. I'll treat you to one if you want."

So here was Kent, not only talking but also accessible. Feeling humiliated and rejected by the fiasco at the print shop, I decided this was my chance to grab myself an escort once and for all.

9

"GET A DOUBLE SCOOP if you want," Kent invited when we were at the counter. It was a hot late-October day, so I took him up on the offer.

Deciding what flavors to choose provided Kent with something to say. I further primed the pump by asking him what classes he was in, and then what sports. He said he'd made junior-varsity basketball.

"I'll come to the games," I said. "My kid brother, Kevin, is a basketball freak and I'll bring him along."

"Great," he said. "We need fans. Nobody comes to JV games."

That was a record nonstop sentence for Kent, so I continued to pry more words out of him. There were some tables in front of the ice-cream store.

Kent looked furtively up and down the street. "It's pretty public," he said, two vertical lines creasing his forehead. "There's a place in the park where nobody sees you."

The park was a couple of blocks past downtown. "We'll be finished with our cones by the time we get there," I said.

"Not if we walk fast," Kent said.

We took off at a rapid stride toward the park, passing down an old street with well-preserved Victorian houses and old-fashioned gardens colorful with asters, dahlias, and chrysanthemums. The fragrance of a giant stone pine that formed an umbrella over the park entrance surrounded us.

"I've never been in this part of the park," I said. Kent was leading the way over the pebbles of a dry streambed whose banks were massed with wild-blackberry vines.

"You ought to come in the spring when the creek is running. And in the summer you can get a whole bucket of blackberries."

The stream led into a stand of redwood trees, where someone had built a picnic table and benches.

"This is it," Kent said. "See, it's private."

We sat down with the remnants of our ice-cream cones. "Why don't you like to be seen?" I asked.

Kent's skin turned a light plum shade and the pupils of his eyes contracted with embarrassment. He was speechless for a while, but I wasn't going to let him get away with it.

"Is it me you don't like to be seen with?"

"If the guys saw me, they'd kid me."

"Kid them back. Tell them if they weren't such jerks, they'd have girlfriends."

Kent looked at me in a strange, disturbing way. Had I just declared myself his girlfriend?

"I wasn't very friendly at the picnic because the guys were watching."

Now that Kent was opening up to me, I felt myself drawing back. Did I want him to be that interested? Yet I couldn't let this moment pass. He seemed to be admitting he liked me. I remembered one of Grandma's sayings, something about striking while the iron was hot.

"Maybe you noticed my grandpa at the picnic," I said.

"I don't know who he is."

"He and my grandma are having their golden-anniversary party in about three weeks. My grandma wasn't at the picnic. She's down in Peru."

"Peru," Kent said. "That's pretty far, isn't it?"

"Clear down at the equator. Grandpa is worried that she won't get back in time, but knowing Grandma, she'll make it if she has to swim. Anyway, the party is going to be a real blast. At that big ballroom at the Elks Club. With a live band and food you wouldn't believe."

"A golden wedding. That's fifty years?"

"Yeah."

Kent gave an incredulous whistle.

I took a deep breath. This was it. I wasn't going to pussyfoot around any longer. The moment had come to pin down an escort for the party, and Kent was at the right place at the right time. He'd just been elected to be it.

"My grandparents told me I could invite one guest to the party so I'll have somebody there my own age," I explained. "I guess I've known you longer than almost anybody else, and I wondered if you'd like to be the guest."

Kent opened his mouth and then closed it again. It took him a while to assemble his reply. "I've never been to anything like that. Would it really be okay?"

"Of course. Like I said, there'll be this great food and a live band to dance to."

"That would be pretty public, and I'm not a dancer," Kent said with an air of defeat. The excitement of being invited faded away.

"No problem," I assured him. "The more people are around, the less they notice you. Besides, I've been taking dancing lessons. Anything you need to know, I'll show you."

"Maybe I will, then," Kent said reluctantly.

I felt let down, now that my invitation had been issued and accepted. I had an escort, but I wished he were more self-assured, had more pizzazz or something. He had talked okay today, but what if he turned silent at the party again? I hoped he was going to do something about his plastered-down hair by the time of the party. Now that I had one, I wasn't sure I wanted an escort.

Nevertheless, I could hardly wait for the ballroom class on Tuesday to tell Stanley that the deed was done. Then I began wondering if my main reason for wanting an escort was to report it to Stanley.

I saw Stanley before the dancing class on Tuesday. He barged into the nursery again when I was on duty.

"I just wanted to get another look at that kid Gabriel. He belongs to Emerald Green, right?"

"Gabriel is a real handful now that he walks," I

said. "We really need an attendant just to chase after him. Want to volunteer? Anyway, get your look quickly, so the nurse won't catch you in here again."

Thelma, who was walking around with a baby trying to quiet it, looked at Stanley, who was sneaking up on Gabriel. Gabriel, in miniature Reeboks, ran from Stanley. He carried a beige teddy bear with a red bow tie in front of him, and the bear was so large Gabriel couldn't see where he was going.

"Whoa, kid, you're headed for trouble." Stanley scooped up Gabriel just as he pitched over.

"Lucky you're carrying that beast as a shock absorber," he said to Gabriel. "Let's get a good look at you."

Gabriel hid behind the teddy bear and gave a shriek of protest.

"Calm down, shut up, and look natural." Stanley sat on a small nursery chair with Gabriel on his lap and pulled aside the fuzzy animal, tossing it to the floor. He jiggled Gabriel up and down, and Gabriel unscrewed his face to give Stanley a curious look. "Da-da," he said.

Thelma and I got hysterical. Stanley gave us a look of mock alarm. "See, he's waiting for somebody to say 'da-da' to," he said. He scrutinized Gabriel carefully, turning him from one side to the other. Then he set Gabriel on the floor and shot out the door.

"What was that all about?" Thelma asked.

"I'm not sure," I said. "But he's up to something."

"Wasn't that Stanley Stoneman, the rich kid?" Thelma asked.

"Yeah," I said.

When Emerald checked on Gabriel at the end of the hour, she gave Thelma and me her usual tongue-lashing, but this time it didn't make me angry, only sad. I could see now that Emerald had had a date with a football player and ended up with Gabriel and a lot of bitterness. I felt sympathy for Emerald. She took good care of Gabriel. He was always well-dressed, and I imagined she must have had to sacrifice a lot of things teenagers value to care for him.

"What was that sudden appearance in the nursery all about?" I asked Stanley as soon as I saw him at class that night.

"I hope I didn't put you on the spot. Confidentially, I wouldn't want to get sued for slander or anything, but those babies without fathers have really gotten to me, especially Gabriel. He's such a spunky kid. He deserves to have a better chance. I've been keeping my ear to the ground ever since I heard that Berglund had been this Emerald's boyfriend, and it doesn't take much brainpower to figure that he could also be Gabriel's father, does it? I've been memorizing Berglund's features and I invaded your space today to check Gabriel out better. I think I discovered some striking resemblances, especially in the curve of their smiles. Have you ever noticed how a smile can be inherited? Have you ever seen Berglund?"

"I don't know him," I said.

"Look him up and see if you agree with my analysis. I thought, here's little Gabriel, just starting out in life, and no father to help him along. When I compare him with me, and the father I've got behind me, I figure his situation isn't fair, and if I've found Gabriel's father, I ought to do something to get them together."

"You're asking for trouble," I predicted. "You saw what kind of disposition Emerald has, and if George is Gabriel's father, she must know it, and one or the other of them must have told the other one to get lost. There must be some reason they didn't stay together." As I said that, I felt a rush of affection for Stanley and his concern for that little scrap of humanity he'd seen in the nursery. Hope welled up in me that he'd succeed in his mission.

It was time to start the lesson, which was going to be a review of the waltz, fox-trot, and rumba. When we got into position, I put my hand a little farther up on Stanley's arm than Mr. Fancher had said was necessary, and I imagined myself in Daphne's shoes, being Stanley's dream girl, pretending I was the one he would be escorting to the cotillion, the one he loved.

"It's a good thing we had a review," Stanley commented when our first shot at the waltz turned out bumpy. "We're already rusty. I keep getting myself into the slinky Cuban position."

"We'll master the waltz again," I assured him, and before long we were swooping around the multipurpose room like native Viennese.

At intermission I told Stanley that I had at last succeeded in lining up an escort for the anniversary party.

"Kent Whitehead!" he exclaimed, thunderstruck. "I had the impression you weren't keen on him."

"Oh, maybe I had some trouble carrying on a conversation with him before, but this last time he opened up some and I decided he'd be okay.''

Stanley continued to be disgruntled. "If I had known you were seriously considering him, I would have looked him up," he said. "How can I give you advice about somebody I don't even know? I checked out Dennis, and in fact I happened to pass by your dad's print shop recently and I got a glimpse of this Bob Holloway, I think. Of course, you can't deduce much about a person just by looking at him through a shop window, but he was good-looking, and he appeared to be energetic and industrious.''

I was speechless for a moment, and then I burst out, "What is this? Some kind of spy job?" I felt a twinge of anger at Stanley's nosiness. "You're missing your calling if you're planning to be an inventor. What you should be is a private eye.''

"What are you getting so uptight about?" Stanley asked. "You've been filling me in on all your negotiations. You wanted my advice, didn't you? How could I give you an informed opinion without doing some research? And now you come up with Kent Whitehead, of all people.''

"Well, you can quit your investigation. I've made a decision, and he said yes.''

Stanley scowled. "My opinion is that you've landed yourself in a can of worms. If I heard correctly, I believe you as much as told Bob Holloway you were asking *him*.''

"It wasn't exactly an invitation." I thought back, remembering exactly what I had said to Bob. "I only told him that after all his work on those invitations he *deserved* to come to the party."

"From a guy's point of view, I would take that as a potential invitation. Your dad came along and interrupted you, right?"

I nodded.

"So it's my guess he's expecting you to follow up."

I didn't want to tell Stanley that Bob had practically made fun of my attempts to invite him. It was time to get back on the floor again. Mrs. Kriek put on a dreary tape, where the singer was complaining about someone's "cold, cold heart."

"And what about Ridge? You also provoked his curiosity by asking him whether he knew how to dance. Then you just left him dangling, wondering what you were getting at. He's probably waiting for you to clarify your comments or explain why you brought the subject up at all. He didn't really get a chance to be considered or for me to give you a complete dossier on him."

"A dossier! Now you are really playing spy. Stanley Stoneman, you've been watching too many TV movies. Why are you making such a big deal of this, anyway? Do you have a file on me, too? What does it matter who I invite to the anniversary party? It's not a till-death-do-us-part type of thing. All I wanted was somebody my own age to be with at the party—a person to hang out with for maybe four hours. You don't understand because it's different with you and Daphne. Once you and Daphne get together at the cotillion, you'll be dating every weekend from then on. I doubt that you can understand a person having just a casual date. Frankly, I don't really care that much about any of these three guys. I just asked the first one I got a chance to ask. I'm sure the others won't die of heartbreak because they didn't get to be my escort. They hardly know me, and besides, I'm not a drop-dead glamourpuss like Daphne Wainwright.''

I'm afraid I pronounced her name with a touch of malice because Stanley said, "You don't need to get sarcastic about it. Anyway, here comes Mr. Fancher to straighten out all the mistakes we made while you were overreacting." His voice became cold. "Let's just concentrate on what we came here for, to learn to dance, and drop the subject of those three jerks."

Stanley resumed the haughty, distant attitude he'd had at the first session of the course, and he didn't ask me if I needed a ride home. I had to beg a lift from Jim and Betty Potts again.

10 ⟿

I REPORTED for day-care duty on the next Tuesday, to be greeted by the usual outburst from Emerald. Emerald and a friend of hers exchanged sneers as Thelma and I walked in the door.

"I should have put a full-length bib on Gabriel. He'll probably barf when he sees who he has to put up with for a whole hour," Emerald said.

"There ought to be a law against exposing little babies to this kind of slime," her companion added.

Thelma and I looked at each other, but kept our silence. We sighed with relief when Emerald and her friend left. But relief turned to alarm when we heard a noisy ruckus out in the nurse's office. We could hear Emerald's shrill voice as she launched an attack against someone she must have hated even worse than Thelma and me. I was further shaken when I heard Stanley's voice being drowned out by the angry and sometimes shocking accusations being shouted outside the door of the nursery.

"I wish we had some earmuffs to put on little Gabriel," I said.

I heard Mrs. Gadsden and the nurse getting into the act outside the nursery, and I tried to hear what was being said, but too many voices were now competing, I peeked into the nurse's office through a crack in the door and I saw Stanley and someone large and burly who I knew was George Berglund. George was backing out of the nurse's office into the hall, shielding his face with his arm. Emerald, with hundreds of tiny black corkscrew curls jiggling around her head, was advancing on George and Stanley with a clenched fist.

"I only wanted to see him, since I heard he was right here at school," George said, not to Emerald, but to the nurse, "but I guess it's not worth the hassle." He turned and vanished down the hallway, with Emerald and her friend in pursuit, yelling threats about what would happen if George returned to the nursery.

Stanley was left in the nurse's office looking confused. I stifled an impulse to rush out and comfort him with a tango clinch.

Mrs. Gadsden asked, "What was this disturbance all about?"

"I've deduced the boy who just left was the father of one of our babies," the nurse said.

"Right," Stanley said. "Gabriel's father. You'd notice the resemblance if you looked closely. I thought that if he saw Gabriel, he might help out taking care of him. The little kid ought to have a chance to see his father once in a while."

"This kind of complication can cause trouble in the nursery, and repeated incidents like this might even cause the school board to cancel permission for day care." The nurse frowned at Stanley.

Mrs. Gadsden gave Stanley a searching look, which turned him defensive.

"Hey, I have no connection with the nursery or any of the kids in there. I went into the nursery one day to talk to a friend, and I saw Gabriel. George was in one of my classes, and I got the idea that it might be good to get them together. But I guess my idea backfired."

"Not necessarily," Mrs. Gadsden said. "You have a point about getting the fathers involved—*if* it can be done amicably. Maybe we could follow up on this, get one of the counselors into the picture." She went out into the hallway, still talking to Stanley, while I explained the fracas to Thelma. I didn't tell Thelma about my connection to Stanley. Why complicate things?

"It does make sense that the fathers should help take care of the kids if they want to," Thelma said. "I'd think Emerald would welcome some extra help."

"The way she welcomes ours?" I said. "Those two must have had a really big blowout, the way she was going after him."

Leaving the nursery later, I saw Kent Whitehead. I couldn't avoid meeting him as we were walking in the same direction.

Kent was tongue-tied when he joined me, and the condition was contagious. We walked a few paces in

111

embarrassing silence, and finally we both said at once, "What's been happening?" There was a round of self-conscious titters before he had to turn off into his biology class.

Maybe Stanley was right, maybe I had invited Kent too hurriedly. We simply weren't comfortable together.

I wondered if Stanley would show up at class that night. There were only two more lessons remaining, both of which would be for review and polishing of our technique. Maybe Stanley felt he was already good enough and had had his fill of a klutz like me. Maybe he was busy enough with the debutante crowd. I felt a stab of bitterness toward Daphne and her rippling golden hair and platoon of admirers. I hated the thought of Stanley groveling and demeaning himself for her attention. I felt grubby and mean thinking these thoughts as I entered the multipurpose room that night.

But the first person I saw when I swung through the door was Stanley. He had obviously forgotten his disagreement with me.

"I hope I didn't get you in any trouble by bringing Berglund to the nursery," he said. "It was rotten luck that he had to run into Emerald, or he might have made a connection with Gabriel. George has never had a chance to see him."

"He admits he's Gabriel's father?"

"Sure. It's common knowledge. It's been eating at him for a long time. But he and Emerald were fighting

112

before Gabriel was born, and she's made it a point to keep him from seeing Gabriel.''

"How did he ever get mixed up with such a witch as Emerald?''

"The way he tells it, she wasn't that much of a witch until she found Gabriel was on the way, and then she really let George have it. Of course, he deserved it. George didn't know Gabriel was in the school nursery until I told him about it, and then George was wild to see him. But he still hasn't.''

"You just brought him at the wrong time. Bring him around when Emerald is in class. Then you might have better luck.''

"That's what Mrs. Gadsden advised, too. But what if Emerald decides to take him out of the nursery and quit coming to school? She seems to hate George enough to do that. I never should have got mixed up with George and Gabriel, only you aroused my sympathy for all those infants.''

A rush of warmth for Stanley took over again and I fought off the desire to encircle him with a giant bear hug. The next-best thing was when the triangle clanged and we took our positions on the dance floor to go through another review of the waltz.

"Have you started teaching your escort how to dance?'' he inquired.

"Not yet,'' I said. "Have you done any practicing since last time? Any more parties with Daphne?''

"Yes, but no dancing. This girl Dee Dee Banfield had a hayride and chuck-wagon dinner out at their farm. You'll be glad to know that I successfully battled Sonny Whitlow so I could be Daphne's dinner partner.

But there were other guys who edged me out in the hayrick to be next to her. Anyway, I did get my fair share of Daphne's attention, thanks to your needling me to be more aggressive. She was really cute. She had on a pink-and-white-checked outfit with ruffles and her hair was done up in pigtails with checkered bows tied on the ends. No wonder all the guys were falling over themselves to get near her. But I still haven't had a complete conversation with her."

"Maybe you will on the night of the big event."

I got a funny feeling as if my stomach was falling into a pit. Just one more Tuesday, and then Stanley would never be my partner again. I glanced at our clasped hands, and pictured Daphne's in place of mine. My hands weren't at their best. I had been helping my dad redo the flowerbeds around the house. We had taken out the faded summer flowers and dumped in fertilizer and peat moss and planted the tulips that always made people gasp with delight when they passed by our house in the spring. I hadn't even polished my nails since we did that job. I wondered if my hands felt rough to Stanley in comparison with Daphne's. Her hands had probably never touched dirt. Anyway, didn't debutantes wear white gloves when they danced? It seemed to me that they did. Maybe he, too, would have to wear gloves. Escorts might, to avoid perspiring on their dates' gowns. I asked if he'd wear gloves, and he said yes. It was hard to think of Stanley in that rarefied atmosphere when he had his arm around me. I felt another pang of envy toward Daphne and something that was suspiciously like love for Stanley.

By intermission the subject of Daphne's cuteness had been exhausted, and he was talking about his invention for the NASA competition.

Maybe I didn't understand the mechanics of the miraculous machine he had devised, but I fully relished the way talking about it animated Stanley. His eyes fiery, the eager words spilled out of him, and he was fascinating and gorgeous.

"Why don't you come out to see it? Maybe after school one day this week. I have it in an old stable at our place. You can even sit on it and get the feel of it, give me your reaction."

I leapt at the chance. "Sure, why not? Tomorrow?"

"Great. I was planning to work on it then."

I met Stanley the next day after school. I was awestruck to be going out to the Stoneman estate. On the way there in the antique jalopy that Stanley told me he had restored himself, a big white convertible passed us going the other way. I got a glimpse of a girl with floating blond hair and a guy grinning at the wheel. Stanley became instantly glum and glowery.

"Do you know who we just passed?" he asked.

"Not a clue."

"It was Daphne and Sonny Whitlow. I wonder where they're going. You see what I'm up against. It's not enough for me to get her attention at the parties. There's all that time in between when I don't know what she's doing, when Sonny, and who knows who else, can muscle in. It's hopeless. All I am is a person on a list who was chosen to get my name linked with hers for one important night. Other than that, she couldn't care less if I exist."

"Hey, don't put yourself down," I scolded. "How do you know Daphne isn't thinking to herself, 'Wasn't that my escort, Stanley Stoneman, who just passed by with some other girl? How come he's two-timing me just a week before the cotillion? I wonder who she is? He doesn't really want to escort me, and couldn't care less about me.' "

Stanley gave a ghost of a smile. "Do you think she saw us?"

"Maybe. You saw her, didn't you? Have you ever shown her your machine?"

"Of course not. That wouldn't be her scene."

"How do you know? If you had asked her out instead of me this afternoon, she wouldn't have been with Sonny Whitlow."

"It's the last thing I would have thought of. Taking Daphne to a mucky old stable? Exposing her to a lot of complicated, greasy machinery? She probably would be bored out of her skin. She's not the type of girl you'd invite to an occasion like this."

How do you think that made me feel? Stanley thought it was okay to toss some grime and technical jargon on a nonentity like me. A sounding board—hadn't he called me that once? Did I remind him of a board compared with the glamorous Daphne? She had passed by so swiftly that I hadn't had a chance to see how curvy she was, but I was getting a few curves myself, or did Stanley even care where I was concerned?

Anyway, that remark about Daphne being too special to go on an expedition where he didn't mind taking me was painful. Stanley didn't seem to notice my hurt, but just went on driving me toward his grubby stable, brooding over whether Daphne liked him.

I had been planning to advise him that if Daphne could see him fired up about his vehicle, she'd be so fascinated that all her other boyfriends would fade into the woodwork. But now that he had put me down, I wasn't going to bother building up his ego anymore. I gave him a resentful sidelong glance and he looked so familiar and dear that I had to forgive him. No matter how he treated me in comparison with Daphne, that afternoon he was mine. It was almost like a date, and I was speechless when we turned down the long, curving drive that led to his house. I hardly got more than a glance at the soaring main house, built of brick and timbers. A fountain spouted in the grassy approach to the wide steps that led up to the massive front door. We took a quick left behind the house, where there were several outbuildings.

"When our house was built, there weren't any cars," Stanley explained. "People had horses and buggies and they had to have stables and carriage houses. Lucky for me, since it gives me work space."

When Stanley opened the Dutch door into the stable, his grumpiness about Daphne and Sonny vanished. You would have thought he was unveiling some king's crown jewels.

"I'm in some science-fiction scene," I exclaimed, viewing a contraption like nothing I'd ever seen before, a collection of jointed aluminum tubes held up by a brushlike structure of dozens of oar-shaped feet.

117

Stanley cast a self-satisfied smile on his weird mechanical daddy longlegs.

"You'll be the first to ride in it, with the exception of me, of course," he said. "A kind of test pilot."

"Does it really run?" I asked, searching for wheels.

"Certainly," Stanley stated. "It may not look it, since it's so unconventional. Instead of wheels it has cilia, like the legs of a caterpillar. But ones that work like oars. Why am I explaining, when you could be experiencing it for yourself? Hop on."

Stanley had mounted a seat on the vehicle, and I climbed aboard, fitting my feet into the stirrup-type gadgets. I felt very uneasy about the machine's flimsiness. It felt as if it wouldn't hold my weight, but surprisingly, it did.

Stanley wore a proud look of anticipation. "Luckily we have a wilderness area out back," he said. "It's a perfect place to test the Paddywhack. That's what I call it."

Stanley had a remote-control unit in his hand, and without warning me, he started the machine on its way out of the stable and down the road.

"It's like riding on feathers," I said. The Paddywhack whispered softly along the road, which led to a hillside that fell off into a creek.

"You can see what a perfect setting I have for testing," Stanley said. He had to run at top speed to keep up with me and the Paddywhack now. The dozens of oarlike underpinnings raced beneath me, a group of them changing angle if they encountered a rock or pothole in the road, so that the ride was perfectly smooth. Yet I felt unbalanced, and had to catch myself to keep from falling off.

"You should have a seat belt on this thing," I shouted. The Paddywhack had outdistanced Stanley, and he was plunging down the hill after me. As we descended, the machine accelerated, hurtling across a ravine and on down toward the stream. Then I found myself going faster than the machine. I catapulted off the seat and fell headfirst into the water.

A stream of curses emerged from Stanley. "My remote control didn't have enough range. Rotten deal! The creek was the main place I wanted to do the test. Now, look! Some of the cilia are bent."

I pushed myself up from the water. My elbow had hit a boulder and was numb. Stanley examined the mangled appendages of the Paddywhack, which was half in and half out of the water.

"Help me get this out so we can see what's broken," he said. That infuriated me. Shouldn't he be pulling me out of the water instead of the Paddywhack? My chin had hit a jagged log and a few drops of blood trickled from the wound.

"How about seeing what's broken on me?" I yelled. I got some leverage on the log and pulled myself to a standing position.

Stanley drew his eyes from his fallen machine to me. "Oh, of course. How thoughtless of me." He extended a hand and I climbed up the stream bank.

"Now we can pull it out. Luckily it's not that heavy. That's what the trouble is—of course. It needs more weight. If it flips over on earth, it will be even less stable on Mars."

"Back to the drawing board," I said. I had heard that somewhere. "In case you hadn't noticed, I'm bleeding. I'm also soaked. I need to go home."

"Oh, sure," Stanley said. "I wonder if Paddy can get back up the hill on his own power."

"Don't expect me to act as test pilot while you find out."

Stanley turned his machine around and pointed the remote-control device in its direction. To his joy, it responded, limping up the incline on its bent oars, while I trudged behind.

"In spite of the accident, I'd say it withstood the test," Stanley told me. "After I repair that one damaged section and add a little ballast, it will be in perfect balance and ready for NASA."

Stanley was paying hardly any attention to me, and that hurt. He wouldn't have exposed the delicate Daphne to a ride on his weird gadget, but I was expendable, hardly worth pulling out of the creek. He didn't even mention my injuries as he was settling his Paddywhack in the stable with tender, loving care.

On the way home he said, "That's just a scratch, isn't it? Lucky that fall was just a slight one, not enough to break any bones. After all, we still have one dance session to get through before the cotillion. I get goose bumps thinking it's only next week when I have to make my big impression on Daphne."

I didn't answer, but Stanley rambled on. "Oh, by the way, it may be a lucky break that you asked Whitehead to the anniversary party after all. I doubt if what's-his-name from the print shop would have been available. I saw him over at the park strolling along with his arm around a cute girl. He's probably tied up with her.''

I was exasperated with Stanley when I finally got out of his car at my house. I seriously considered skipping our last class.

11

BY THE NEXT WEEK I had my sense of perspective back and knew I couldn't miss my last dance class. Maybe I had let myself get a little too attached to Stanley, so that his casual remarks hurt my feelings. But I had known all along that he was learning to dance for Daphne. And hadn't he made it clear that Daphne was his first love? I had seen for myself that the Paddywhack was his second, and that I was only a way to get through the town recreation program's ballroom-dancing class. Maybe we'd had a little fun in the process, gotten along well, and maybe he'd benefited from the moral support I gave him in his pursuit of Daphne. But now I had to face facts. The episode of my life with Stanley in it was coming to an end.

These calm and rational thoughts were driven away by loud screaming when I passed down a hall near the nurse's office. It was Emerald Green in another rage,

122

and I could imagine that George Berglund couldn't be far away.

I could hear babies crying as the nurse's door burst open and Emerald, her face distorted with anger, plunged out, holding Gabriel tightly against her.

"I'm taking Gabriel home!" she exclaimed. "I thought he was safe here, but now they let this creep in to spoil everything."

"Spoil! Who's spoiling anything?" Big George Berglund lumbered out the door to confront the furious Emerald. "I got permission from Mrs. Gadsden to come in and see him. She thought it was a good idea for me to help take care of him."

Emerald caught sight of me and her anger shifted across the hall. "You're the one to blame. It was your boyfriend who dug George out from under the rock where he's been hiding for the last year and sent him over here to interfere with Gabriel just when we were doing okay."

Mrs. Gadsden made her appearance from the home-ec class next door. "It's my doing, Emerald. When George came over last week, I talked to him. He told me—didn't you, George?—that he'd like to make it up to you and Gabriel for running out on you."

"Yeah. It was too scary, and too much of a shock when I first heard Gabriel was on the way. I couldn't cope with it, and I tried to pretend I didn't have anything to do with it. Then Stoneman, over in metal shop, tells me he's seen Gabriel right here at school and that he was exactly like me, and when I saw him, well, it really got to me and I knew I ought to take some responsibility for him."

"I told you I never wanted you to see him, and that's the way it would have stayed if these busybodies hadn't ganged up to try to get Gabriel away from me. What I'm going to do is call the police and tell them to keep you away from him."

"Now, Emerald." The nurse was standing beside Mrs. Gadsden. "Nobody is trying to take Gabriel away. We're all trying to help. George wants to help, and for Gabriel's sake, you have to let him try. Won't this little tyke be better off with two parents than with one?"

"Some parent. Totally ignored both Gabriel and me up to now."

"I told you. Up to now, I couldn't cope, but now that I've seen him, I could put in part of what I get pumping gas on weekends to get stuff for him. Food and whatever."

"Why don't we all go into my office?" the nurse suggested. "The school psychologist will be in this period, and we could discuss it with her."

"Now they'll get us royally messed up," Emerald protested. "Setting a shrink on us."

"Mrs. Gadsden said I have certain rights," George argued.

"Rights!" Emerald exclaimed. "All you've done to me and Gabriel are wrongs!" Her flashing eyes cast a malevolent dart my way before they all left. Gabriel was starting to fuss.

The girls who had been on duty in the day nursery had come out to hear the altercation. "It'll never work, not with Emerald's temper," one of them said.

"It will take us the rest of the hour to quiet these babies," the other one predicted.

It seems that when a day starts out confused, it continues that way for the remaining hours.

For instance, at lunchtime, who should be waiting at my locker but Kent Whitehead, looking as if he wished the floor would open and swallow him up.

"Hi, Kent," I said.

He gulped and shifted from one foot to the other.

"How's it going?"

"Okay, I guess, only . . ." He began to stammer, and no more words emerged.

"Well, it's a little less than a week till the anniversary party," I reminded him.

"I know," he said. "That's the trouble."

"What trouble?"

"We have a preliminary exhibition game."

"A what?"

"The basketball team. At Whittington High."

"That's nice. I hope you win."

"But the thing is . . ." Kent became tongue-tied again.

I stood in front of him and forced him into major eye contact. "Okay, out with it, Kent."

"Our game is Sunday night. They don't usually play on Sunday night, but the varsity was using the gym on Saturday and—"

"You mean you can't come to the party?"

"If I don't play in the game, I get kicked off the team."

"Oh, great! So you're canceling."

125

Kent put his palms up in a helpless gesture. "There isn't any other choice."

So I was back to square one, without a partner again. Now my choices were limited to Bob Holloway and Dennis Ridge, and only five days left till countdown. But after Stanley's sighting of Bob with a cute girl, I could cross him off my list. So that left Dennis.

"I'm not going to the anniversary party with Kent after all," I announced to Stanley when I arrived at the last dance class that night.

"How come?"

I explained about the preliminary game.

"Oh, well, you're not that keen on him anyway." Stanley seemed jumpy. His eyes were glittery, and they darted nervously around the room. While we were waiting for Mrs. Kriek to give us the gong, the foot on the leg that was crossed over his other one bounced up and down, transferring his nerves to me.

"Is something the matter?" I asked. "You seem hyped up."

"I guess I am. It's only four days until the cotillion, and this is my last chance to get good enough for Daphne. I keep imagining that I'll mess up, you know, tromp on her little white satin shoes, step on the hem of her dress and rip it, bang her up against somebody else on the floor."

"Stanley Stoneman, I'm ashamed of you. If you drag yourself down with that attitude, you *will* do all those things. You still have the assets that made you her escort, so you want to strut in there and flaunt yourself. She's lucky to have you for a partner. You're a great-looking guy, especially when you smile. Smile a lot, maybe a sort of condescending smile, to show her she's the one who's got the prize. And you're a coordinated, terrific dancer. You haven't trampled on me, have you? We're experts, right?''

Stanley brightened a little at my efforts to raise his morale, but not much.

"Number one, Daphne didn't pick me for her escort. There's this lady, the social secretary of the cotillion, who put together the couples. Just grabbed us out of thin air, mostly according to who our parents are, because we're teenagers, and not anybody ourselves yet. That's how we got stuck together. Maybe she did me a favor by putting me with Daphne, who's not only beautiful, but has a sweet disposition, too. The only thing I can complain about is that these other guys hang around her all the time.''

"Forget them. Once you're her official escort for the evening, she'll see what a really great guy you are. She'll tell the others to get lost.''

The gong sounded and Mr. Fancher summoned us to the dance floor. Stanley's fingers curled perfectly into my down-curved ones. His arm slid around me, I realized with a twinge, for probably the last time. My hand traveled up his arm and rested on his shoulder. We would go through all our repertoire that night, close together while Stanley polished up his act for Daphne. We were a well-integrated team—even the tall couple commented that we should enter a contest.

Stanley smiled at me when he heard that. "We did okay.''

"We're going on with the advanced course. What about you?" they asked.

We both shook our heads and our eyes met briefly. "Our mission will be accomplished this week," I said. "After that, we may never be in a ballroom again."

"So, Whitehead had other plans," Stanley commented later, after the intermission. I guess he was feeling sorry for me a little because I had such a hard time getting a date.

"I guess I'll have to make a last-minute invitation to Dennis after all. Which is only logical, since he's the one who knows my grandparents."

Stanley gave a stormy frown. "I hate to tell you this, but Dennis Ridge has a reputation as a ladies' man. I've been checking up on him, and I doubt that he's a suitable date for somebody unsophisticated like you."

"But you said that I owed it to him to follow up on my hint to him about knowing how to dance."

"Maybe so, before I knew anything about him." Stanley twirled me out and then back into his arms, looking down at me with a stern, big-brotherly expression.

"But it's either him or going with my kid brother, Kevin, which isn't an acceptable alternative."

"Don't say I didn't tell you to proceed with caution where Dennis is concerned." Stanley pulled me closer when Mr. Fancher changed the music to a tango. We swooped and gyrated, and my heart did a dismal flop when Mr. Fancher turned off the music for the last time.

"Well, this is it," Stanley said. "Nobody could say we didn't do our best."

Betty and Jim passed by. "Good-bye, Richard," Betty said. "Nice work, Linton," Jim added.

Stanley looked embarrassed. "I didn't need that fake name," he said. "Nobody cared who I was."

I tried to conceal the bleakness that overcame me, knowing our last dance was over. "Good luck at the cotillion," I said a little hoarsely. "Show those other guys who's in charge of Daphne."

"And, hey, have a blast at the anniversary party," Stanley said. "Remember my advice about Ridge."

The Caribbean couple drove away. The couple who were going in for contests waltzed across the courtyard, his arm around her. Jerrolyn and her beanpole partner passed by separately. They had made it through the course. Mrs. Kriek and Mr. Fancher stood outside the multipurpose room conferring for a minute before going their separate ways. Mr. Fancher carried the tape deck and a little case holding the tapes. Mrs. Kriek's triangle dangled from her hand.

I heard Stanley's homemade car sputter away. Then I was alone and waiting for Grandpa. Maybe I'd see Stanley around school from time to time, but it wouldn't be the same as when we'd been partners every Tuesday. My throat became full. My eyes teared.

Grandpa roared up to the curb and his brakes squealed. He was in a snit, which he explained to me on the way home.

"We're in a real pickle. I had a message this evening that your grandma is stuck up in that Tambopata River place. It seems they've had heavy rains that have swelled the river and washed away the canoes they were going to use to leave the wildlife refuge. There's no way they can get out."

"Rain can't last forever, Grandpa." I tried to cheer him up. "Somebody will go after them."

"We've got a deadline here. More than two hundred people are invited to an anniversary party where one-half of the golden wedding couple won't be present."

"She still has a few days," I reminded him.

"I warned her not to push her luck."

"Grandpa, if Grandma doesn't get back in time, I'll be your partner."

"Here she is, clear across the equator. And only five days till the party. Maybe it's all right to have an adventurous spirit, but you have to quell it now and then when it interferes with other people's plans. Especially when there are hundreds of them involved."

I didn't want Grandpa to be on the outs with Grandma when they had already gotten through fifty years with each other. But I just let him rant and rave. He needed to let off steam. By the time we reached home, he had exhausted his frustration, and I had been thinking my own thoughts. It was really too late to teach Dennis Ridge to dance if he didn't know how. What did Stanley mean about a ladies' man? Just that he ran after a lot of girls? I would have been one of them if Grandpa hadn't come home the day I was washing windows.

"What we ought to do is just cancel the party. Let

everybody know your grandma has gone off on some wild tangent and everything is off.''

"It would be too hard to get ahold of everybody by Sunday, Grandpa."

"I'll have your dad print up a batch of fliers. We'll mail them out. 'Because of the impulsive nature of Lavinia Royce, who is stranded in the Peruvian jungle, the Royces' golden anniversary party is canceled.' ''

"Oh, Grandpa," I said. "What if she makes it out of Peru, gets back, and finds you canceled the party? Or what if the fliers didn't reach the guests? You know how Mom is always complaining about the slow mails? Tomorrow is Wednesday. We wouldn't get them out till Thursday at the earliest, and they wouldn't reach people in time. They'd get all dressed up and come to the party and find there wasn't any. Then they'd all be mad at you."

Grandpa ranted on until we reached home. My mom fixed us a snack and calmed Grandpa down a bit.

"Of course we'll have the party," Dad said. "We've rented the hall. The caterers have probably already bought the food by now. It's too late for the band to get another gig. Anyway, Dad, it'll still be your golden wedding anniversary whether Mama is here or not, and everybody who knows you will want to celebrate it."

"On with the party," I said.

Grandpa grumbled away and went to his house to bed.

Kevin was still up. "I'll give you another lesson in the fox-trot," I said.

131

Emily Hallin

"That stuff is useless," Kevin said. "Anyway, all I'm planning to do is eat at that party."

I put the tape in the slot, and at Mom's urging, Kevin agreed to take a turn around the family-room floor. I'd have to draw the line at the waltz and the fox-trot—I'd never be able to guide Kevin's overgrown feet through those intricate South American steps. "Slow, slow, quick quick," I chanted, just like Mrs. Kriek. Kevin's eyes rolled up in his head with disgusted resignation. "After all, you and I may have to be partners at the anniversary party," I said.

"Phooey," he answered.

Actually, I was still considering the possibility of Dennis Ridge. Too late to teach him to dance, maybe, but it might be possible to give him some on-the-job training at the party in case he didn't know how. We could get off in some corner and I could display my expertise to him. He was okay looking. Actually, with that blond hair, he was very attractive. Once we got acquainted, who knows where it might lead?

I didn't have much time, so I stalked him. But got nowhere. Then I used Stanley's method of going to the school office to check on his schedule.

I waited in the vicinity of the metal shop for him to emerge. But Stanley came out before him, and he spotted me across the hall.

"The countdown is on," he said. "Only three days till the big event. Do you think we're ready?"

"Sure," I said. "You'll be sensational." A lurch of loss shot through me to hear his voice and realize that our days as partners were over. He was on his way to Daphne.

132

"How's your bash progressing?" he asked.

"Disastrously." I told him about Grandma's dilemma in Peru and how we had considered canceling the party.

The bell rang and we separated. As Stanley turned from me I felt a part of myself being pulled away. It was like a big roller of surf crashing over me, batting me into the sand. I couldn't believe that I had totally flipped for Stanley.

I saw Dennis Ridge at the metal-shop door and my emotions were too intense to ask him then. I hurried in the opposite direction, my mind hopelessly hooked on Stanley. Scenes of Stanley hauling his Paddywhack out of the stream, and of his confronting George Berglund with his son, Gabriel, in the nursery whirled through my thoughts in waltz time, syncopated into a rumba, and haunted me through chemistry class, mingling with symbols and formulas to put my mind into a spin.

The next time I saw Dennis he was ducking into the boys' room, so I had to put off asking him indefinitely.

12 ∼

THE DAY BEFORE the party, I alternated between eating my heart out imagining Stanley preparing for the cotillion and fussing over my mopey grandpa. Grandpa had received another message from Grandma a couple of days ago saying that they had obtained canoes to travel down the river to a place called Puerto Maldonado, but there was incessant rain there and airplanes couldn't land because there was no control tower.

"Maybe it's stopped raining by now."

"Even so, when she gets out of there, she'll still have to catch another airplane to get back to the United States. She won't have any reservations, and we'll be lucky if we ever see her again."

"Oh, Grandpa, of course we will."

Mom had gone out to do the weekly grocery shopping, and Dad was working on a rush job. I hated to leave Grandpa alone in his depressed state, so when he said he was going out to check on the refugee farmers, I offered to go along. I kept up a stream of distracting chatter, but Grandpa remained glum. The scene at the farm didn't improve matters. We were having a drought, and the crops weren't doing well. The gnarled Oriental farmers weren't as gloomy as Grandpa. They hacked with a patient, resigned attitude at the weeds that stole the scant moisture from their vegetables. Now and then they conversed in their strange singsong tones. They had to carry water from a well in buckets to the plants.

"I'm afraid the well is going to run dry," Grandpa said. "Then we'll be in for it."

"The farmers don't seem worried," I observed.

"They're so accustomed to hardship that they don't react anymore," Grandpa said. "I never saw a year to equal this one for bad things happening. Why couldn't we have a little of that rain that's stranded your grandma?"

"It doesn't seem fair," I agreed. "But Grandma isn't going to stay in South America forever. You have to get it together and enjoy the anniversary party. I'm your date, okay? We're going to move and shake up a storm." I confessed then that instead of Japanese brush painting I'd been in a ballroom-dancing class. "I did it just to surprise you, Grandpa, and it was a lot of work, so I'm counting on dancing with you."

Grandpa was touched by that news and he brightened up a bit.

"And when Grandma comes home," I suggested, "we'll have another party to tell her what the golden wedding anniversary was like. A friend of Dad's has a video camera. He's going to take some movies of the

party, and Grandma will feel that she was there. We'll
show her how you carried on even while she was
stranded."

A mischievous gleam illuminated Grandpa's eye.
"Show her the old man can hold his own on his fiftieth
anniversary without her."

"That's the spirit, Grandpa."

When we returned to Grandpa's house, Dennis
Ridge had already put away the lawn mower and left.
Anyway, by then I had given up the idea of having an
escort. The chances that Grandma would return were
approaching zero. I'd settle for hanging around
Grandpa and dancing with Kevin, trying to develop
some social graces in that little savage. Although
Kevin seemed to have twice as many knees and elbows
as Stanley and was three-quarters of a head shorter
than I, I did manage to teach him a few basic steps,
and I could already envision party guests viewing us
on the dance floor and whispering, "Aren't they cute?
That's Milford's granddaughter and grandson."

Though I kept up a continuous effort to build Grandpa's morale, my own spirits took a nosedive when I
looked at the Sunday paper on the morning of the
anniversary. One section was loaded with pictures
from the cotillion. And right in the middle were Stanley and Daphne. She was looking up at him, hanging
on to his arm (the same one that had encircled me at
the ballroom class). Stanley hardly looked like the
same person I knew in jeans and shirt. He had
on formal gear with a white tie and a big victorious
grin on his face, indicating that he had followed all my
instructions and had succeeded in wowing Daphne.

He had attained his goal, while I hadn't even had the gumption or finesse to get myself an escort. Weird as it seems, a nonentity like me had helped make Stanley into a dazzling star of the cotillion. The curtain had opened for Stanley and Daphne now, and I was still hidden in the wings. I would have moped about it if I hadn't been so busy that day. A lot of gifts had come for Grandma and Grandpa and it was my job to open them and write down what the gifts were and who sent them.

Grandpa complained about that. "It's darn foolishness for people to send gifts to a couple that's been hitched for half a century. We already have so much junk we can't close the closet doors. I thought we were saying on the invitation, 'No gifts.' "

"We did, Grandpa, but if it pleases people to give you presents, you have to accept them. Grandma will write notes to all these people when she comes home."

"*If* she comes home!" Grandpa was getting grumpy again.

Thelma broke up the day by asking me to get a burger with her for lunch, and I'm glad she did, because what we saw was incredible. Thelma and I couldn't stop gaping.

Seated at one of the tables were Emerald Green and George Berglund, who was holding little Gabriel on his lap. Gabriel was gurgling and brandishing a french fry. Emerald and George were actually laughing.

"They look like a family," Thelma exclaimed.

"I hope they are. Little Gabriel needs a father, Emerald needs something good to happen to improve

137

her disposition, and you know who's responsible? Stanley Stoneman. Stanley was the one who got George interested in Gabriel.''

"Stanley's almost human," Thelma said.

I gave Thelma a glare. "People have been misjudging Stanley. He might be the most human person in school.''

"He's a big society star now. I saw his picture plastered all over the *Chronicle* this morning," Thelma said. "He didn't look so stony."

A lump came to my throat and I dropped the subject.

"I wish you could come to the anniversary party tonight," I said, "but it's only family and Grandma and Grandpa's friends. It will be just me and Kevin and all those senior citizens.''

Thelma walked back with me and helped me log gifts. Mom and Dad were over at the Elks Club, supervising the decorations and the table settings. Kevin acted as if nothing special was happening. I could hear him grinding raucously on the driveway on his skateboard until he came in with the knee of his jeans torn and a bloody kneecap emerging.

Thelma is one of those people who hate the sight of blood, so I lost my assistant logger. I sent Kevin to take a shower before I bandaged him.

"You'll have to stay in your room until the party," I ordered. "It's only a few hours away and you could get into more trouble."

"You can't make me dance now, not with this knee." Kevin seemed triumphant. I had a fleeting suspicion that he might have crashed off his skate-board on purpose.

Kevin had the shower going full blast and was splashing so loudly that at first I didn't hear the car pull up in front of Grandpa's. Then I heard Grandpa shouting and a lot of commotion, which drew me out of the house.

There was Grandma, her safari slacks scruffy and rumpled, her jungle hat askew, scrabbling in her hand-bag for fare for the cabdriver, who was hauling her rain-stained duffel bags out of the trunk.

"Lavinia, why didn't you phone me?" Grandpa asked.

"Did try, from Los Angeles. Nobody home."

I had dashed to their house by now. "That must have been when we were out at the farm. Grandma, I can't believe you made it."

"You didn't think I'd miss my own fiftieth-anniver-sary party? Maybe I had to act a little ornery down in Lima so the airport officials would get me out of there. But here I am, no worse for the wear."

Grandpa had his arm around Grandma. "You really feel like going through with the party after your or-deal?" he asked.

"What ordeal?" Grandma said. "I napped all the way up here. I have so much to tell about. We got a glimpse of the quetzal along the riverbanks below Machu Picchu."

"Mom and Dad will flip when they see you," I said. 'They're over finishing the decorations for the party. Wait till you see all the presents you got."

"She can't see them now," Grandpa said, herding

Grandma toward the house. "This lady has got to be cleaned up so she'll be presentable at the party."

"It's been a long time since I had a hot shower," Grandma acknowledged. They went in their house and I ran to mine, calling to Kevin that Grandma had arrived home from South America.

"All right!" Kevin responded. "That ought to get Grandpa over the grumps." He was wrapped in a towel and still needed his knee doctored.

I ran to the phone to call the Elks Club. I wanted to be the one to tell Mom and Dad that Grandma was back and was going to make it to the party. While I was on hold, waiting for somebody to find one of my parents, our doorbell rang and I heard the towel-draped Kevin limping to answer it.

"She's on the phone," I heard him say, and just then Mom answered and I told her the good news. After a few exclamations of delighted surprise, she told me she and Dad would be home soon to freshen up for the party.

Then I turned to see who had rung our doorbell. I was face-to-face with Stanley Stoneman and totally speechless.

"I just happened to be passing by your house and I remembered this was the night of your party and I was curious about how it was turning out."

I turned stammery. "Better than we expected," I said. "Grandma just got home from South America a few minutes ago."

"No kidding? And your party is definitely on? You didn't take those grueling ballroom lessons for nothing?"

Stanley was grinning his familiar grin at me, and was his old self, in jeans and sweatshirt.

"It's going to be a major event, but I don't know how much ballrooming I'm going to do. After I taught this kid all we learned, he had to go and smash his knee, which I have to doctor."

Stanley followed Kevin and me while I went to get the antiseptic and a giant Band-Aid.

"You mean you settled for going with your kid brother?"

"The party seemed so iffy, I thought an escort would only be one more problem. Especially one I hardly knew."

"But now that everything is turning out okay, you probably could use an escort."

"It's too late now. I'm just planning to get in my dance with Grandpa and blend into the woodwork."

"But I was thinking as long as you haven't invited anybody and I'm not busy tonight—in fact, I still have my rented monkey suit—I could fill in as an escort if you wanted me to."

Strangely, that gave me a fit of laughing. Kevin was all ears, looking from one to the other of us.

"Is it so hilarious to have me for an escort?" Stanley's voice had an injured tone.

"No, of course not, only I'm surprised you're concerned about me after the big event last night."

"Is it okay with your grandparents if I come?"

"They'd be delighted."

"Then I'll go home and change and be back. Okay?"

"Are you sure you want to do this? You don't have to, you know. I was going to do all right on my own."

"As hard as we worked on those ballroom lessons, we ought to take every opportunity to use them."

"This may be our last chance. Mine, at least. You'll probably go to a lot of balls."

Stanley's face twisted into a strange grimace as he departed.

"Yah, yah! Megan has a boyfriend," Kevin taunted.

"Don't be ridiculous," I exclaimed. "He was only my partner in the dancing class." But I had a curious churned-up feeling that Stanley was acting suspiciously like someone who cared about me. A lot. And after his long-awaited big night with the glamorous Daphne Wainwright. Stanley was a surprising guy.

It was complete confusion in our house when Mom and Dad raced in to change their clothes and Kevin and I were getting ready. Stanley's unexpected invitation caused me to glow and made me look better than I usually do. I had a new party dress, and when I had wiggled into it, I felt touched with a special sparkle.

Stanley commented on it, too, when he reappeared in his formal outfit, looking like someone from the movies. He whistled, took my hand in the arch-turn grip, and twirled me around for inspection.

"This can't be my everyday partner from Kriek and Fancher's ballroom class!" he exclaimed.

"I'm afraid so. I turn back into a pumpkin at midnight," I said.

Stanley put that well-known arm around me and gave me an intimate, tingly squeeze as we went out to his car. "If I'd known you were going to be so elegant,

I would have brought one of Dad's cars instead. I reconstructed this car myself, but now it doesn't seem worthy of the occasion.''

"It's great," I said. "A Stanley Stoneman special. An original.''

"I hope you didn't think I was forward, inviting myself to your party."

"I'm surprised you'd remember this party after the spectacular event last night. I saw your picture in the paper with Daphne. She looked properly impressed."

Stanley didn't comment on that. It wasn't far to the Elks Club, and he was soon parking the car.

"Grandma didn't want to have a receiving line. She just hopes the guests will mingle informally."

"Good idea," Stanley said.

"I hope you realize that we'll be the only teenagers here."

"Sort of like the ballroom-dancing class. I'm going to miss those Tuesday nights," Stanley said.

"Me, too," I agreed. I cornered Grandma and Grandpa and introduced Stanley. He quizzed Grandma about her trip to South America, and was interested to know that the sun plummets into the horizon at exactly six o'clock in the evening every day of the year at the equator.

"Stanley is about to be a scientist," I explained.

The band was tuning up. It had one of those wild, head-tossing drummers, and their warm-up sounded disturbingly like rock music.

"Grandpa, this is a rock band!" I protested.

"It's time we got in touch with the 1990s," Grandma said. "I thought our fiftieth anniversary would be a good time for Milford and me to learn these newfan-gled dances. We don't have much more time.''

"But, Grandma, Stanley and I have been taking lessons for ten whole weeks, expecting music like 'The Anniversary Waltz.' We're all primed for it.''

"Lavinia, Megan did this as a surprise for us," Grandpa said. "Let's tell them to change tempo. Frankly, I don't think I could stand those decibels for a whole evening.''

Grandma, after taking in the expectant looks on my face and Stanley's, agreed. Grandpa went to the band-leader, who shrugged and the musicians shuffled their music around and soon produced "The Anniversary Waltz.''

Grandma and Grandpa swooped onto the floor. Grandpa had rented a tux and Grandma had on one of her old evening gowns. A big lump came in my throat, and even my dad's eyes sparkled with tears.

"May I have this dance?" Stanley asked with a comical bow after my grandparents had completed a circuit of the ballroom. We joined Grandma and Grandpa on the dance floor, and then Mom and Dad followed us and there was a lot of clapping and cheer-ing from the other guests.

"It feels just right to be dancing with you," Stanley said. "Last night, I felt something was missing. It was you. Daphne seemed to resent it when I'd try to adjust our handhold. I kept wishing Mr. Fancher was there to show her the correct procedure. She'd sometimes miss my signals. I'd be thinking, 'Where's Megan, now that I need her?' One of Daphne's troubles was she was always rubbernecking around the room to see what everybody else was doing, who Sonny Whitlow was dancing with, or where her girlfriends were, and that would cause us to bump into other people and she'd give me this look like I was some kind of bumpkin. I kept comparing her with you, missing you. It wasn't important anymore whether Daphne liked me or not. And I didn't care that much about dancing unless it was with you. We're just natural partners."

I masked the excited thrill of hearing Stanley say that, and tried to act cool. "It's just that we learned together. The cotillion was a little disappointing, I take it."

"A lot disappointing. Of course, I got to see that spectacular procession, where these girls in their long white dresses come out with their bouquets through that arch to meet their fathers. Daphne's father, when he was finished dancing with his daughter and he handed her over to me, said, 'Oh, so this is Stanley Stoneman's son,' like I was in some kind of freak show."

I put my hand farther up Stanley's arm, clear up to his neck, in fact, and an almost inaudible, satisfied sigh came from somewhere inside me.

"I have a confession to make," Stanley said. I saw Mom and Dad waltz by. "You know when I told you I saw Bob Holloway out with this cute girl? I never saw him at all. I had got used to the idea that you were my partner, and I hated the idea of your inviting such a good-looking guy to this party."

"That was a sneaky thing to do."

"And I might as well finish telling you what a total scoundrel I am. All those things I told you about

Dennis Ridge were made up, too. About him being a ladies' man. I doubt if Dennis has ever been out with anyone, and the way you described it, he seemed to like you. I was afraid he'd make a rush on you, and I guess, subconsciously, I had designs on you myself. All along I think I wanted to be the one you picked for an escort, and I finally got up the nerve to appoint myself this afternoon. While I was driving over to your house today I was afraid you might have grabbed somebody at the last minute, and I'd be too late."

"But you gave me the impression you'd flipped for Daphne."

"Maybe for the notion of her. But I didn't really know her, and when I was finally with her, I kept wishing for you, remembering our dancing lessons, how I could trust you to ride the Paddywhack, and the new things I learned because of you. Like about the day nursery. Did you know that George Berglund and Emerald Green are going to try to get together and raise little Gabriel as a family?"

"I saw them down at the burger stand, and they looked pretty close."

"That made me feel good. Also, I talked to my dad about that day-care center. I told him how they didn't have enough space for the nursery, and you know what? My dad said he was glad I had developed an interest in some social concerns, and that he'd contribute a portable classroom to the school for the nursery. Besides that, he's looking into setting up nurseries in the companies he's involved in so the mothers who work there can keep an eye on their kids."

"I never thought our Tuesday-night conversations

would lead to all that," I told Stanley. "Maybe I'll forgive you for lying to me about Dennis and Bob."

After Mom and Dad had danced with Grandma and Grandpa, and then my uncles and aunts had done so, I claimed my dance with Grandpa. It turned out to be a tango, and I had to teach him as we went. It was comical.

When I was with Stanley again I said, "I've figured out that I was only talking about getting an escort for this party to make an impression on you. All along, you were the escort I wished for, and my wish came true."

"You would have been fed up with Bob or Dennis or Kent before long anyway, as I was with Daphne," Stanley said. "We were both hoping for a fantasy world, when we were involved in the real thing every Tuesday night."

"Right," I agreed. "As you said, we're just natural partners."

Stanley gave me his illuminated grin and guided me out to the hallway, where we indulged in a few kisses, and that seemed even more natural yet.

About the Author

Well-traveled and an avid bird watcher, Emily Hallin is the author of more than 25 young-adult books. The only girl among four boys, she grew up in Colorado, then later moved to Missouri, where she attended the state university. In later years, she worked at Stanford University, where she came into contact with the many young people who have inspired her work. Ms. Hallin's next book will be *Changes*, the second in the series about Meg and Stanley.